H[O]
AROUND
AGAIN

Other books by Don Coldsmith

Horsin' Around (Naylor, 1975)
Trail of the Spanish Bit (Doubleday, 1980)
Buffalo Medicine (Doubleday, 1981)
The Elk-Dog Heritage (Doubleday, 1982)

HORSIN' AROUND AGAIN

by
Don Coldsmith

Foreword by Kurth Sprague

Corona Publishing Company — 1981

Copyright © 1981 by Don Coldsmith
All rights reserved. For information
address Corona Publishing Company,
1037 South Alamo, San Antonio, Texas 78210.

Library of Congress Catalog Card No. 81-67743
ISBN 0-931722-13-6 (cloth)
ISBN 0-931722-14-4 (paper)

Cover illustration used with permission
of the Appaloosa Horse Club
Additional drawings by Paul Hudgins

Printed and bound in the United States of America

Foreword

"There's something about the inside of a horse," runs the old adage, "that's good for the inside of a man." Or, for that matter, woman, girl, or boy.

It's a belief of mine that there exists a unique freemasonry, a singular comradeship, among horse people that has nothing to do with sex, age, where they live, how much money they have, what kind of saddle they ride, or what breed of horse claims their affections: All unite in admiration of the horse.

Being around horses, it strikes me, is an ennobling experience: horse people have more humanity than other kinds of people. Evidently there's something very good about having to take responsibility for creatures so much larger and more powerful than we are, and who depend so utterly upon us, their masters, for their very existence. And in undergoing this happy slavery we find ourselves becoming attuned to things eternal: we center ourselves in the swing of seasons, we are newly-receptive to the glory of nature. Even the old homely chores of feeding, mucking out, and grooming help us to be more tolerant, more apt to find within ourselves the ancient virtues of patience, reliability, and conscientiousness.

Reading this book confirms me in these cherished beliefs.

Horsin' Around Again — a compilation of Don Coldsmith's *Horse, Of Course!* magazine columns about horses and horse people — is a safe bet to prompt in delighted readers of all ages smiles of joyful recognition ("*I* had a horse that could do that once!") or twinges of rueful recollection ("Same darned thing happened to *me* when I tried that!"). All, however, will be grateful that these tales have been gathered in one book.

Now Don Coldsmith is a practicing physician and, as one might expect of a doctor, his mind is keen and analytical, his perceptions sharp.

But he's also a horseman who knows that while, yes, there's a lot of science to looking after horses, at base horsemanship is still — thank heavens! — in large part an art, an art often concealed in mystery. Why is it that what works with one horse won't work with another?

Respect for individuals is a very useful trait in dealing with people; it's a necessity in dealing with horses. Don Coldsmith's readers will detect at once that he's an exemplar of this virtue. But more than commending him for this, we should praise him for his disarming candor in admitting that he, too, has made mistakes with horses. *That* kind of endearing honesty's in short supply anywhere, and is rare indeed coming from a horseman!

Kurth Sprague
Blackacre Stable
Austin, Texas

Table of Contents

Foreword by Kurth Sprague
Introduction

Horsin' Around   11
Stormy
Late Snow
The Muckledun Bay
Year of the Horse
Outlaw
The Pint-Sized Stallion
Spring Cleaning
A Matter of Preference
High Country
Missy
Yard Full of Horses
Somethin' New
Mom's Horse
The Mothering Urge
The Escapees
A Boy and a Horse
One More Winter

Horse People   47
Suicidal Tendencies
Rosie

An English Saddle on the Prairie?
Dad
The Elder Statesman
Nuyaka
Dudes and Tenderfeet
The Trophy We Don't Have
Charlie Crouse
Grandpa
Tom Bass
The Lazy SOB
The Folk Hero
Ready for the Ring?
"Dark-Skinned People"
The Small-Animal Man
The Natural-Born Rider
The Centenarian
Red Cloud
The Expensive Cure

Nostalgia Ain't What It Was   *89*

A Winter Adventure
Butch Cassidy's Yard
Real Cowboyin'
New Year's Party
Run, Spot, Run!
Dining on Horseback
Jim Key, the Educated Horse
Runaway!
Code of the Cowboy
The Mountain Wedding
Pony Express
Black Jack
Sidesaddle
The Sole Survivor
The Left Hind Quarter
When the Work's All Done

Animal Tales — 125
Wilful Disobedience
The Trophy Hunter
A Dog's Best Friend
The Passing of Ten Point
The Baby-Sitter Cow
The Reasoning Process
One of the Family
Dog Tales
Blue Lightning
The Foster Mother
A Heck of a Nose
The Settin' Hen
Instinct or Understanding?

Gatherin' Sunbeams — 153
"Let's Pertyke"
Hunting Season
The Classified Ads
The Gentle Art of Profanity
Ghost Horses
Mixed Team
The Federal Outhouse
The Self-Milking Cow
T. Hamilton Bone
Nature's Fertilizer
The Cribber
Aesop's Horse
The Tractor Speaks
How They Get the Milk Out
The Thirsty Phantom
The Grass is Greener

Introduction

Ten years ago this fall "Horsin' Around" started. (Actually, horsin' around had been going on for a lot longer than that, but I'm talking about the column.) Each week since that time has produced a new article, carried by a variety of newspapers around the country, and reprinted in part in the monthly magazine *Horse Of Course!*

It's been fun. I've met a lot of wonderful people, heard and retold a lot of good stories, and gained a lot of writing experience. (After all, you can't do anything five hundred times without improving at least a little.)

Our five kids, who were small in the early columns, are pretty well grown and gone. A couple of them are married, and we're now grandparents. Edna is still my best friend, most trusted critic, and she still laughs at my jokes.

We've phased down some on the horse breeding program. When there are no kids around to help with chores, halter-breaking colts, and all, it's just too much work. So we keep just a few horses around, breed a few outside mares, and raise a handful of beef cattle on our hundred-odd acres in the tallgrass Flint Hills. And, I'm still writing.

Once in a while someone will tell me about an elderly relative who enjoys the "Horsin' Around" articles, but who is scandalized by the title.

"I'll bet he doesn't know what that means," chuckled one delightful little old lady to her daughter. She thought the whole thing was deliciously naughty.

Well, I did know what it meant, grandma. "Horsin' ", or "horsin' around," originally meant strictly sexual activity. A mare in season and ready to accept the stallion's attention is said to be "horsin'." Likewise the stallion, when he perceives that the mare is interested, will squeal and strut around and put on quite a show. This, also, is called "horsin'."

Now, a couple of generations ago, any reference to sexual activity of any sort was taboo. Even the word was hush-hush. Therefore, any words which had to do with such activity were simply not used in polite conversation. People or animals, it made no difference. The thing was to ignore the existence of sex.

Gradually, the term "horsin' around" came to be used as a description of any boisterous, show-off, possibly aimless activity. Like the flamboyant stallion who's just putting on a big show. Now the expression has assumed the proportion of mere nonsense activity. Except, of course, for a few people of an earlier generation.

Words do change their meaning through usage, or in different parts of the world. "Ranch", for instance, in our part of the country, implies at least a few hundred acres. But it's not only size that makes it a "ranch", but produce. A ranch produces livestock, and an operation producing plant products is a "farm", regardless of size.

Elsewhere, it's different. In California, a couple of acres of nut or fruit trees is a "ranch." There are a lot of fruits and nuts in California.

This thing of word usage does turn up constantly, as readers or editors become accustomed to ranch-country language. Sometimes it's good for a chuckle, or for a whole column.

In 1975, a collection of 100 articles was published under the column's title, *"Horsin' Around."* The volume was well received, but it is now out of print, and there have been inquiries about another volume. (Well, my brother, somebody at the feed store, and a lady who types for me asked about it.)

This volume is the result. Another gathering of the best articles, including those which drew the most comment at the time of first publication. They're grouped in general topics, but you can read them in any order you want to, including back-to-front. A few have been updated, altered, or rearranged, to eliminate confusion, and to make them fit better into the more permanent format of a book.

Enjoy, and I'll see you down the road.

Don Coldsmith
Emporia, Kansas
July 1981

HORSIN' AROUND AGAIN

Horsin' Around

Stormy

One of our most memorable horses is an old mare named Stormy. We bought her for our daughter April, after the death of her first horse, Lady, and an unfortunate experience with another young mare in between. Stormy turned out to be the horse we should have had all along.

Her name doesn't refer to her disposition, but to the fact that she was born on a dark and stormy night. She was three when she came to us, a beautiful coppery sorrel, with a white star on her forehead. Stormy is an unregistered "grade" animal, but shows some evidence of breeding. She's put together like a well-built quarter horse, with some indications about her head, the set of her tail, and the fine thin skin that she may have some Arabian blood in her close background.

She became an ideal family horse. She did give me a slight problem once, soon after we bought her. I was home for lunch and as I started back to work, noticed that the kids were having a little trouble. They and a visting cousin were riding Stormy. The horse had discovered that she could "take the bit" and, ignoring their best efforts on the reins, she would amble back to the barn. The kids were becoming pretty discouraged, and I knew it was bad for the horse to get away with this. I stopped, walked over to the pasture and crawled through the fence.

"Here," I said, "I'll take that out of her for you!" (Well, I was younger and in somewhat better shape then.) I stepped up, not even bothering to adjust the stirrups, and gave Stormy a good kick in the ribs to get her attention. I got it. The mare started a series of short bucking crow-hops down the pasture, jarring my teeth, and legs and loose stirrups flopping wildly. She bucked for 50 or 60 feet until she came to a puddle of mud from the night's rain. It was the only damp spot in the entire pasture, and Stormy crow-hopped right up to the puddle, put her head down, and stopped short. I sailed over her head and landed spread-eagled in the mud, while the horse just stood and looked at me.

I got up and climbed back on, and the horse handled perfectly! I rode back up to where the kids were sitting on the top rail of the fence, and turned her back over to them, and she again was the perfect animal for inexperienced kids! Apparently our little escapade impressed Stormy as much as it did me, because she has never bucked or given anyone any trouble since, as far as I know. Of course, I did have to change my wet and muddy clothes, from the skin out.

Stormy is so reliable that we have no qualms about putting completely inexperienced riders on her. The mare will look after them.

Stormy "talks" to us. When anyone is around, she is constantly making small nickering noises, asking for attention. April, when she was small, used to say Stormy would talk to her and tell jokes to her. Maybe she did. The jokes weren't much, though.

One of the mare's most endearing traits is her mothering instinct. She has had several foals for us, all above average quality. Some mares are very secretive and defensive about a new foal. Not Stormy. When her foal arrives, she brings it up to the fence near the house and stands there calling to us until somebody comes to look. She pushes the little fellow toward us with her nose, talking softly, while we pet him and get acquainted. I'm never sure whether she's showing him off to us, or vice versa. Maybe both.

Horsin' Around

Late Snow

The late coming of spring has caused a few problems for gardeners, who haven't been able to plant according to the *Old Farmer's Almanac*. It has also been a problem for cattle and horses which were ready to give birth when the weather wasn't right. A lot of ranchers have lost calves from the late storms.

Early in April we had a late "winter" storm warning, with the livestock advisory from the weather bureau and all. We had a couple of mares nearly ready to foal, so I thought I'd better take appropriate measures. We had one stall available in the barn, big enough for a mare to give birth in, so I got both animals in and examined them to see which might be closest to foaling.

Both had milk in their udders, but neither had the waxy discharge from the nipples that usually heralds the approach of labor. One mare seemed to have a bit more fullness in her udder, so I just left her in the barn, fully realizing that neither mare would probably foal that night, anyway.

The storm moved in, dumped four inches of snow on the whole area, and moved on. Next morning the sun came up bright and cold against the new snow, and the mare in the barn hadn't foaled yet. I hadn't really expected her to.

We had breakfast, watching the other horses behind the house, as they nibbled hay and warmed themselves in the rising sun's rays. I finished my coffee, put my coat on, and prepared to leave for town, when suddenly my wife called excitedly from the kitchen. I had already opened the door to leave, but came back in to see what the emergency was. She pointed to the expectant mare in the pasture. The mare had calmly laid down in the breakfast hay, and her sac of waters had burst, right before my wife's gaze, signaling the start of labor.

I stepped out across the snow to see what I could do. A mare progresses very rapidly in labor, unless there is a problem, and will usually deliver within 20 or 30 minutes. One foot of the foal was already showing, and the mare nervously got up, lay down for another contraction, and repeated the process. I was trying to stay back and not excite her, but also trying to keep the other curious horses and our old dog, Spot, away from the little mare. I'm sure we were all bothering her.

Suddenly she got up, heaved a long sigh, and started across the snow toward the pasture gate. Good, I thought! If I can get her through the gate, I can lead her in, to foal in the loose hay on the barn floor. I crawled through the fence and ran down to meet her at the gate. I got there first, and opened the gate for the mare, as she ambled clumsily along. Both front feet and the foal's nose were visible now.

The mare almost reached the gate, then stopped, lay down, and gave another mighty heave. The foal popped out on the snow, a tangle of long legs, umbilical cord, and sac. He blinked at the sunlight, snorted, and shook his head till his ears flopped like an old hound fighting flies. I treated the stump of his cord with antiseptic, and dried him with a handful of hay. In an hour he was on his feet and happily nursing, and by evening he was loping in circles around his proud mama.

I'm always astonished at the miracle of birth. In spite of all our feeble efforts to help, nature has the entire process pretty well figured out, and does well in spite of us.

The other mare, the one in the barn? As I write this, she hasn't foaled yet. She will when she's ready, I guess. I hope it's not in the snow.

The Muckledun Bay

We were sitting in the grandstand one evening in summer, watching a county 4-H horse show. It was a pleasant evening, cool, and with a light south breeze carrying away the arena dust. The nicest part of the evening for us, though, was watching our Connie, now 14, ride one of our horses. And the nicest part of that, in turn, was that she was doing well in some pretty tough competition. I mean she was winning a little.

Now, I've always emphasized to our kids that it isn't the winning that's the important thing, it's the participation. She has thoroughly accepted this principle, and she's a good loser. She's had a lot of practice. Unfortunately, to be a good loser, you have to lose. We've done our share of that in the show arena. As the saying goes, we've won and we've lost, and winning is more fun.

The announcer called the name of Connie and her horse again, and she went over to receive another ribbon. I was proud of both horse and girl, which brings up another story.

This horse was born on Friday, January 13, 1967, in our barn. Naturally, a foal born on Friday the 13th had to be called "Lucky." She was a special colt, product of a new bloodline for us, and eagerly awaited. With her champion ancestry, I thought sure we'd have a winner. The foal was a little disappointing. She was a trifle small, and her right front foot turned out just a bit. Her mane and tail were as curly as a buffalo robe, and her ears, instead of standing upright, sort of drooped to a horizontal plane, sticking out like the wings of an airplane. Then, too, I had hoped for a foal we could show. The January birthday should have given us a big husky show colt by horse show season. And Lucky didn't even have enough color contrast to exhibit. Appaloosas aren't a color breed, but they do have to have enough to be recognizable to the public. Otherwise they are registered "for Breeding Stock" and cannot be exhibited. Lucky was a sort of an odd mousey color, a muckledun bay. We couldn't exhibit her.

As a yearling, the filly began to show white snowflakes, and eventually became a nice Appaloosa roan. (She kept her fuzzy mane and tail. That's still somewhat of a problem.) I'd watch her in the pasture, and could see that she moved well, was intelligent and quick on her feet. Her ears still stuck out sideways, however.

When she was two, we had a local trainer break her to ride. He was quite impressed with her and predicted that she'd be a great performance horse.

Now, a new problem. I couldn't get any of the kids interested in riding her. I approached April, our oldest, horsiest daughter.

"Honey," I pointed out, "she's likely to be the best performance horse we'll ever own. You could *win* with her!"

"Dad," she'd answer, "I just don't like the way she works. Besides, she holds her ears funny." (I have since been told, this shows good cow sense.)

I tried with a couple of the other kids, and they'd make a halfhearted effort, but not really try very hard. In spite of this, Lucky brought home a couple of wins for them.

Then Connie, our youngest, came along. She was finally big enough to graduate from her small first horse to a full-sized animal. I cautiously suggested Lucky. Connie was dubious. She'd seen her older sisters either turn the horse down, or bungle the job. Finally she decided to try it with Lucky, and after a year or so of hard work, she began to show some results. This has been the best year yet for both horse and girl.

Lucky is nine, now, a bit old for a start on the competitive circuit, but she seems to thrive on it, and should have several good years yet. She and Connie are a great team.

The show ended, and I met Connie at the gate by the trailer. She had what looked like an armful of trophies and a red, white, and blue halter that was for all-round high point winner.

"Gosh, Dad," she said, "that was sort of embarrassing."

Honey, your old dad can use a little of that sort of embarrassment once in a while.

Year of the Horse

I recently received, by a rather roundabout series of events, an interesting newspaper clipping. It was sent by a regular reader, a retired army colonel. This professional soldier at one time commanded a horse-drawn battery of field artillery, and was impressed with the horses, their intelligence, and their capability in their jobs. He also made a point in his letter of the love that developed between the teamster and his charges.

In looking through some of his mementoes from a tour of duty in Japan, the Colonel had run across an old clipping, entitled "Year of the Horse." He was kind enough to send it to me.

The clipping is from a Japanese newspaper called *Mainichi*, and is dated Friday, January 1, 1954. It is a feature story by "Narao Matsumoto, staff writer." Fortunately, the article is in English. I don't read much Japanese. The occasion for the article was the change of the year in the old Japanese zodiac calendar. 1953, it seems, had been the Year of the Serpent, and Matsumoto was writing his article in observance of the start of 1954, the Year of the Horse.

Having lived in Japan, I was aware, to some extent, that the horse figures prominently in Japanese mythology and folklore. I certainly was not aware of most of the interesting little anecdotes that this Japanese writer mentions.

One of the earliest mythologic references to the horse is that of Prince Susano-o, who brought the skin of a horse and flung it into the Royal Palace. This may be a remnant of some story involving the first actual contact of the Japanese with these animals.

There is the story of a mystic dragon-horse which lived in the Kiso region, unseen by human eyes. When finally seen by a mortal, the dragon-horse disappeared into Heaven. There he "sheds his hair down to earth" in the form of rain or snow when thunder and lightning occur. Incidentally, storms with thunder and lightning, as we know them in the middle west, appeared to me to be very rare in Japan.

There are stories of the faithful horse which shed tears at losing his longtime owner, and of a horse which avenged his murdered master and friend, after a particularly brutal killing.

Horse stories abound from the Japanese feudal age. The *samurais*, professional fighters equivalent to the knights of Europe, rode superb horses into battle. Two valiant warriors are said to have competed on horseback against each other for the honor of being the first to cross the Uji River under enemy fire to attack the foe's positions.

Fearless samurais rode down the bluffs of Ichinotani in another famous battle, taking the enemy by surprise. The bluffs had been considered impassable. This area is now part of the city of Kobe. I've seen the bluffs in question, and I sure wouldn't want to ride a horse down them!

One story quoted in the article is Chinese in origin, about an old man named Tsai, who owned an excellent stallion. One day the horse disappeared, and the friends of Tsai all lamented the loss.

Tsai was philosophic. "The misfortune may turn out to be a blessing." Before long the stallion returned, bringing with him a fine mare. People rejoiced, but not Tsai. He felt this blessing might somehow disguise misfortune.

Soon after, his son, riding horseback, fell and broke his arm. People expressed sympathy, but Tsai only smiled and said again, "This may turn out to be a blessing!"

It was not long before an enemy invaded the province, and the young men were conscripted to fight the invaders. All except the son of Tsai. He was excused because of a broken arm!

Outlaw

Of all the horses we have raised, sold, traded, or used, very few have ever tried to buck or kick. We have felt that this is because most of ours are handled from the time they're born and understand human contact. There was one notable exception.

A few years ago we bought a couple of mares from a friend who was moving to town. One was a big roan mare that I had admired for years, and she was obviously very pregnant. Less than a month after we brought her home, she delivered a beautiful male colt, just the sort any horse breeder dreams of. We started to work with him at about one day old. The kids named him "Scout." He developed well, seemed more intelligent than average, and at the appropriate age was trained to saddle. Here was a better than average gelding for performance or competition showing, or just for using. I put a pretty high price on him, and waited for the right buyer. Meanwhile, the kids rode him, one of our daughters took him with her for a few months at college, and her boy friend even roped with him a little. Scout continued to act like an alert, intelligent animal.

Finally, when Scout was four, the right buyer did come along. A young woman, looking for a horse for competition, saw and fell in love with him at first sight. She was an experienced rider and liked the way he moved and handled. The price was right, and we delivered the horse a few days later, everyone satisfied. For the time being, that is.

In a couple of days she phoned me, fairly sputtering with anger. Through the profanity, I managed to understand that "that blankety-blank horse blankety-blank near killed me! I thought you said he was broke!" I couldn't believe we were even talking about the same horse. She had taken him out for a workout, and after 20 or 30 minutes, had tried to push him into an extended canter when he suddenly began to buck! Not just the little crow hop many horses will do, but as she described it, a "bawlin', squallin', rodeo buck", squealing every time he hit the ground. She stayed on about six jumps, she said, then unloaded fast and hard, and watched as the horse "bucked for another hundred yards, bawlin' every jump!"

Just to make sure, she had ridden him again the next day, and Scout had repeated the performance, dumping her even harder. Well, no way out of it. We made the hundred mile round trip to pick him up, and refunded her money.

Now, what to do with him? We located an experienced young horsewoman who was doing a little training and she agreed to try to ride the bucking streak out of him. He piled her on her face, fast and hard, and she agreed that he did act like a bronc out of the rodeo chute, grunting, squealing and all.

I was telling a rancher friend about our problem, and he offered a solution. He had a hired man, he said, who could ride anything with hair on it. Let him work with the horse awhile. We hauled Scout down to the ranch.

The next time I saw our friend he had quite a tale.

"Don," he said, "I've seen horses of all kinds for sixty years, but I never saw anything like him! He *does* buck like a rodeo horse out of a chute!"

I ventured the thought that I might try to sell Scout to a stock contractor for that purpose, but he hastily continued.

"Oh, no! We sort of like him! When he gets the buck out of him every morning, he makes a pretty fair sort of a cow horse. I'll trade you a load of hay for him!"

I jumped at the chance, and Scout is now a working cow horse. They still have to watch him, however. He bucks out in the morning, and "sometimes after you get off to open a gate and then get back on."

I'll never understand why an apparently well-trained horse suddenly turned outlaw. But they tell me he is making a pretty fair cow horse.

The Pint-Sized Stallion

There's never a dull moment for people living in the country. If it isn't too wet or dry or the cats having kittens, it's something else. Like old Spot tangling with the skunk the other night right outside the screen porch. The kitchen was a bit rank for a day or two. I'm sure Spot thought he was just doing his job. At least, he seemed pretty proud of the fact that he had repulsed the intruder. The vice versa part didn't seem to occur to him.

Not long ago we were just watching the news and weather and about to turn in when Connie came sleepily down the stairs.

"Dad," she said, "I think there's a pig in the yard! I hear it squealing!"

Well, no one near us has any pigs, but stranger things have

happened. I got a lantern, pulled on boots, and stepped outside. I could sense a bulky shape shuffling along the fence and heard a piglike squeal, but couldn't get the light on the animal. It looked very dark, and was shaggy and too big for a pig. An uneasy thought about bears crossed my mind for a minute before I got the lantern beam full on the creature. It was a miniature pony! Moreover, it was a stallion, and the squealing we had heard was this pint-sized visitor trying to explain to our big mares in his shrill falsetto that he was the greatest stud-horse in the world. They looked a little confused about the whole thing, and were pretty agitated and nervous, crowding the fence and trying to see what was going on. Our old stallion was sort of confused, too. He bugged his eyes out and leaned over the fence to get a better look at this strange creature. I was afraid some of them would break a fence down out of sheer curiosity.

Well, now that I knew I wasn't going to accidentally rope a bear in the dark, I didn't mind trying to catch the visitor. As soon as I had a rope on him, he quieted down and I led him to the barn, put him in a box stall, and looked him over in the light. The stallion was mature, but very small, probably less than 36" at the withers. He was a pretty little fellow, a dark, almost purple chestnut color. The head was well shaped, he had good feet and legs, and was sleek and fat.

I fed him, and went inside to discuss the situation with the family. Mom and Connie were still laughing at the silhouette they had seen as we crossed the lighted barn door. They hadn't known what I had on the rope, but saw me pass the door, followed by the lariat, with the half-pint on the end.

We talked it over. None of us could think of anyone with ponies near by, and we'd certainly never seen this one. We called a few neighbors, but no one had any better idea than we did.

Connie, who doesn't think much of ponies in general, was of the opinion someone had "dumped" him. People dump unwanted dogs and cats in our area sometimes, she reminded me, so why not a pony? This gave occasion to mention that dumping unwanted animals in the country is a cruel and dastardly trick, anyway, but that people just don't dump a pony. I finally realized she was teasing me.

We had the little squirt about three or four days. We advertised on the radio and in the paper, and called everyone we could think of that might know who was missing a miniature pony stallion. He wasn't much trouble, and certainly didn't eat much, but he was a nuisance. We couldn't turn him out with our horses, because he would start acting like a stallion around the mares. The sheriff was investigating, but could find no reports of a missing stallion. I was about desperate enough to consider Connie's idea.

Finally we had a phone call—the grapevine filtered down and some people a mile or so away who hadn't missed their pony from the pasture yet discovered an open gate. They picked him up and we were back to normal. At least, what passes for normal around our place.

Spring Cleaning

This is the time of year when the horses are shedding their winter hair and growing sleek and shiny for the season. When Connie, our 14-year-old, comes in from riding or working around the horses, she seems to be surrounded with a cloud of fine soft fur. It clings to everything and generally makes a mess on clothes if you're not careful. You have to brush off or change clothes before sitting on the furniture, so this becomes a house rule, especially at this time of year.

Most animals have a tendency to shed winter hair after they no longer need it for warmth. Birds "molt", or change feathers, and some actually change color. This is especially true in the far north, where snowshoe rabbits and ptarmigans are white for protective coloration all winter, but change to brown in summer.

There are probably several factors which signal for the change to start. One is temperature, of course. A few warm days like we had in late February this year will start the shedding process.

Another is light. The increasing percentage of light hours to darkness, about 12 of each as I write this, signals for a lot of springtime changes to take place. Birds fly north, and start to stake out nesting sites. Even domestic birds feel this. We keep a light bulb burning all winter in the chicken house to fool the old hens into thinking it's summer so they'll lay more eggs. It works.

It must be very confusing to dogs and cats that are kept inside all year, with both light and heat in steady amounts. We have some friends who used to warn us when we prepared to visit them, "Heidi's shedding!" Heidi, their German shepherd, was kept in the house. It seemed like she was shedding about seven times a year. I'm sure her coat never quite figured out what was going on.

Connie tells me she is planning to keep her mare in the barn for a few weeks. This mare has a tendency to grow longer winter fur than some. As the show season begins in only a few weeks, it becomes advisable to try to get the winter's growth cleaned off. Otherwise, when we enter the ring for the first couple of shows, all the other people's horses will look sleek, shiny, and well-groomed; ours will look like a motheaten bear rug.

There are several methods of accomplishing this early shedding. I've noticed a time or two when we had an expectant mare in the barn to await foaling, that her coat would start to shed in only a few days. We have also kept a horse blanketed to create artificial warmth and induce shedding. I recently heard a suggestion that a 100 watt bulb, burning in the horse's stall 24 hours a day, will cause shedding as well as a blanket. That's the light-dark ratio again. Probably a combination is the answer.

One thing is certain. When they start to shed, they really shed, all at once. This is particularly noticeable with a light-colored horse. They will lie down in the corral, roll around and scratch their back, sides, and belly against the ground. Shedding must be an itchy process. Then, when the animal gets up, there's a circular patch of light fur on the ground, sometimes in big clumps. The first time I saw this happen with an old buckskin mare we had, I thought it was frost, or some strange fungus, until I went out for a look. Wish there were some way to recycle and utilize all this fur.

One day I came home to find one of the girls grooming her horse with a currycomb. Great handfuls were lying on the ground and more bunching up on the comb. Obviously, the horse was at the height of seasonal shedding.

"Hi," she called, "I'm doing my spring horsecleaning!"

A Matter of Preference

We've had several "outside" mares this spring to breed to our stallion. Caliente Bayberry, better known as "Bubba" to the family, has, in fact, been busier than any year so far. And again, it's a matter of great interest to me that a stallion has definite preferences. I've noted before that our old stallion, Huckleberry, preferred sorrel mares over any other. He disliked light-colored mares. Intensely so. Huckleberry once chased a light roan filly right through a wire fence. Fortunately, most of the damage was to the fence and not the horses.

Huckleberry's very favorite mare was an ancient, ugly, old bony sorrel. She may have been a sort of mother figure for him, I don't know. But he'd be as gentle and docile as a lamb any time that old mare was around. Sort of curious, though. His mother wasn't a sorrel, but a dark bay roan. He also liked a black mare of ours quite a bit.

Bubba has similar tastes. He's perfectly content when the same big black mare is around. He likes sorrels, too. He's established a good relationship with a big buckskin mare that has been here for a while to breed. And he likes our Appaloosa mares.

I guess it's perfectly logical for them to have preferences of this kind. (After all, people do, too. I'm sort of partial to blondes, myself.) It may be that some past experience dictates this preference, in horses or in people. Maybe, for instance, Huckleberry was once kicked by a light-colored horse and hadn't gotten over it. This would explain his anger and his chasing of the light roan filly.

One of the visiting mares to Bubba this year was white. I doubt he'd ever seen a white horse before, and he just didn't seem to know what to do about her. The mare was very receptive, strongly "horsin' ", and Bubba just ignored her! He seemed to be aware that he was supposed to be aroused, but he couldn't believe this white mare was the source of his interest. He'd look at her, become interested, and then sort of wander off to look at some dark-colored horses in another lot. He thought *they* were the cause of his arousal.

I was talking not long ago to an experienced horseman who was visiting from out of town. We were discussing this point of stallion preferences. He wholeheartedly agreed with me, had seen his own stallions do the same thing. And he told me a story that may indicate the past experience theory is valid.

It concerns a nationally known stallion whose name would be familiar to anyone acquainted with that particular breed. This animal was standing at stud to a large number of outside mares. One of them was a good buckskin mare of nice quality. It so happened that the stallion had never been around many horses of this color, but it didn't seem to bother him any.

Unfortunately, at the height of the breeding frenzy another variable was introduced. The mare, not familiar with this corral, happened to touch her nose to the top wire of the fence. An electric fence. Both horses received a pretty good jolt, and the stallion went straight up in the air and over backwards. He'd have nothing more to do with that mare.

In fact, I'm told, for the rest of his life, nothing could ever persuade him to breed a buckskin mare. Can't say I blame him.

Horsin' Around Again

High Country

Last year our daughter April and her husband moved to an area near the Colorado-Wyoming border. Mike is in a ranch manager's job and they are looking after about a thousand cattle in a cow-calf type operation.

April had intended to take a mare of hers out there to use, but that animal turned up unexpectedly pregnant, so it wasn't too practical. I suggested that she take Raspberry, one of our old original Appaloosa mares, to use for the summer. She has ridden Raspberry in shows, parades, trail rides, and various competitions for years. The mare had never worked cattle, but they needed one mostly to ride fence, check stock, and didn't intend to rope from her or use her for cutting. This seemed like a good solution so we loaded the mare with Mike's horse in their trailer, and they started west.

A minor accident on the highway skinned up the leg of Mike's cow horse before they got back to the ranch, and it became apparent that the horse wasn't going to be used much that summer. They did need a horse, however, so Mike decided he'd try Raspberry. He worried some about the altitude. They were at slightly over 7,000 feet above sea level, and the mare had spent all her life at our lower Kansas elevations. However, she seemed to acclimatize well and to enjoy working cattle. Before long Mike was roping from her, and she could hold the toughest steer or cow with little difficulty. He began to appreciate the mare. I thought this was pretty amusing, since he had teased April so much about the animal.

He did lose his temper with Raspberry once. Mike had stopped to fix fence and the mare wandered off. He had to walk about a half mile to find her, and was pretty irritated when he finally located her peacefully grazing among the aspens.

"I decided to ride her down till she'd be too tired to wander off!" he told me.

For the next hour or so, they ran up and down the high country meadows, which is no mean trick in the thin mountain air. At the end of that time, Mike related, "*I* was too tired to wander off, and Raspberry looked like she was just startin' to get warmed up!"

This increased his respect for Raspberry, but he and the other cowboys continued to tease April about the mare, calling her "Gooseberry" and making fun of her long nose and ears. (Okay, I never said she was the *prettiest* horse in the world.)

Still, after the injury on Mike's horse had healed and he was usable again, they continued to use Raspberry to work cattle. I noticed on a recent visit out there that even the teasing that went on showed a great deal of respect and admiration for the animal. One of the part-time cowboys told me aside that he'd have more confidence in Raspberry to hold a big steer on his rope than any horse but one he'd ever used.

Mike volunteered that he didn't think the mare had ever been completely tired out. That's quite a statement, considering how hard a horse is used in working cattle, especially in the high country.

Well, I've always maintained that a horse should be a *using* horse. We have tried to develop animals that would be useful for any one of several different major endeavors. Here's Raspberry, used as a show horse, trail horse, performance competition, and brood mare, and she has been relatively successful at all of these. Then, at middle age, she learns working cattle, and handles that well, too.

I was very pleased to hear one of the cowboys ask our daughter, "April, when we move the cattle off the ridge next week, can I borrow Raspberry?"

We must be doing something right.

Missy

While sorting out some stuff from my dad's estate recently, we came upon a letter he had saved. It's short, and in a childish scrawl. The date is Sunday, May 27, 1962.

"Dear Grandpa and Grandma Coldsmith,
Thank you very much for the $2.00. For my birthday I got a sorrel yearling. Her name is Missy. I paid $23.77 for her and daddy and Mommy paid the rest. Her Grandmother one 1st in the American Royal, and her mother one 2nd. Well guess I better go.
              Love, April."

We thought it was interesting that he would have saved that little letter all these years. It brought back a lot of memories for us.

May 27, 1962, was April's tenth birthday. Just a short while before, her first horse, Lady, had died. Lady was just two years old, but they had a sort of understanding, and were the finest team of child and horse that I ever saw.

Lady died very suddenly, and we were anxious to replace her. April wanted to contribute all her savings toward the new horse, so we agreed to pay the difference between $23.77 and the sale price. We looked at a lot of horses, and finally decided on a nice sorrel filly. She was immediately named "Missy" by the delighted April.

Missy looked quite a bit like Lady, with similar markings and the same bright coppery color. That was one of the reasons for choosing her. Another was that I thought she looked like a pretty good filly. Her mother was a beautiful, registered American Saddle Horse, and her sire a quarter horse. That looked like a good cross to me. Besides, there was the information mentioned by April in her letter. This filly came from a family of winners. We settled back to watch the delightful horse-and-girl relationship blossom again as it had with Lady.

Boy, were we surprised! Missy proved to be an entire new experience. She was moody and irritable. Sometimes, I was ready to concede, even mean, evil, and a number of other things I couldn't call her in front of the children.

She was hard to catch. We'd have to corner her in the stall, and even then, if we didn't get her head under control in a hurry, she'd turn and try to kick us. This was a far cry from Lady, who would run to April to be petted when she called.

I figured that this trouble was just because the filly had never been handled much. Patience, kindness, and firm discipline ought to bring Missy around. So we tried. For weeks and months, we tried. April would sit on the stall and talk to Missy while the filly ate, and by the hour try to pet the animal. Then suddenly Missy would bite or kick at the girl. I guess we were pretty lucky the horse never connected solidly.

Instead of improving, Missy became worse. She would lay her ears back when anyone came into the barn. April came to me with tears in her eyes. "Daddy," she sobbed, "I love Missy, but she doesn't love me!" I tried to work with the horse, and finally had to give up. I had never seen a horse act like this. We hired a young man who was a pretty good trainer to work with her.

After a few get-acquainted sessions, he saddled the filly (by this time, two years old). Missy waited until he got on, then took off like a bronc out of a chute, to put it mildly. She bucked for several jumps before she unloaded the rider, and then ran away. She ran through a stout cedar rail fence. *Through* it, not over. Kindling wood flew everywhere. We finally ran her down and got the saddle off and the fence fixed.

After a few more sessions like this, the trainer gave it up as a bad job. This, he told us, will never be a kid horse. It would be best to sell her, and he knew where we could find a good, dependable animal to replace her. We jumped at the chance, and bought Stormy, who is still with us, and one of the family.

Missy? We sold her, very cheap, to a young man who knew her problems. By very patient effort, he finally rode her a little. She was still moody. Then one day, he noticed a swelling on her head. The vet suggested taking her to the Vet School at Manhattan, but there was nothing they could do. Missy died from a brain tumor.

I felt very sorry about the new owner's loss, but somehow, I felt better. It was a comfort to know that that unpleasant year wasn't our fault, or Missy's. She wasn't mean or evil, she was sick, and in pain. I was glad it was over for her.

Yard Full of Horses

One morning recently I awoke just before the alarm went off and lay there sort of waiting for it to happen. Spot was barking, and I supposed he had discovered a skunk or a possum or heard a coyote. Then suddenly I heard the unmistakable sound of a horse's squeal. It didn't sound like one of ours. You get so you sort of recognize the "voices" of your own various animals. I jumped out of bed and looked out the window.

I should have listened more carefully to Spot. He had been trying to tell me something, and his information was pretty important. The front yard was full of horses and donkeys. It looked like there were a dozen or more, milling around and grazing on the lawn. It was almost full daylight and I could see that none of them were ours. There were all sizes, shapes, and colors, some ponies, some pretty good looking stock horse types. I could also see, as I yanked on pants and boots and charged out, that our fences were down in a couple of places.

I headed for the barn. My first concern was that our stallion might be loose. I sure didn't want him out there initiating hostilities and injuring somebody's horses. Or breeding anybody's mares, for that matter. People get a little unreasonable about things like that sometimes.

The fence of his corral was broken at one point, but for some unexplained reason he hadn't done anything about it and was still inside. I shut him in a stall in the barn and breathed a little easier.

By this time I had recognized some of the horses in the yard. They belonged to a neighbor about a mile away. In fact, three or four were horses we had raised. That explained what they were doing here. They had come home. We've had that happen before—horses coming "home" as far as two or three miles, and years after they left our place.

Back in the days when everyone used buggies as a means of transportation, this was a very useful characteristic. A tired traveler, nearing home, needed to pay little attention to the road. The horse would take care of the driving. A person with a dependable old horse, in fact, might even be able to catch a nap during the trip. And imagine the advantages to a young couple courting. The driver not only didn't need to watch the road, but he had both hands free.

A reader once wrote me about a horse they had when he was a child. The horse was stolen, broke loose, and came home — nearly thirty miles, they figured, from where it had been seen. This included *through* a couple of towns.

Frank Dobie and Will James both wrote about horses that returned to areas that had strong memory ties. In one case, it was many years later. As I recall, a mare sought out a cactus patch where she had lost a colt, and spent some time calling for her lost youngster.

I wasn't particularly thinking this sort of thoughts at the time. The herd had gone around the house by now, and were squealing at our horses across the back fence. I was afraid they'd spook and run out into the road, so I cautiously edged around and opened the gate to an empty corral. One of the leaders saw the open gate and trotted in, followed by the entire group.

Meanwhile, my wife had sized up the situation and called the owner. I was fixing fence when he drove up, sleepy-eyed, with a couple of his kids. Somebody had left the gate open, he said. Without much trouble, he caught the "boss hoss" of the bunch, put a halter on him, and started home leading him. The rest of the bunch followed meekly. Of course, this leader was an animal that came from our place originally, and had led the others "home."

There weren't really a couple of dozen, like it seemed originally. Only nine or ten, and one old donkey. In retrospect, it was a sort of funny and interesting episode. Just the same, I'd hate to start every frosty winter morning that way. And I'm sure my neighbor agrees.

Somethin' New

A few years ago we sold a horse to a youngster, a family friend. It was a pretty good type of a horse, a young gelding. The boy was relatively inexperienced but had ridden some. The horse was a bit more than green-broke, and was gentle and cooperative. It was a classy-looking animal, and I thought this had all the makings of an ideal combination of boy and horse, for anything he wanted to do.

I was surprised and disappointed a couple of weeks later to get a phone call from him. He was having trouble. When he'd try to saddle the horse, it would shy away, buck the saddle off, and go completely nutty. This didn't even sound like the same horse we'd sold him. I went over to see what was the matter, and he met me at the pasture.

As soon as he lifted his saddle out of the car, the horse started to fidget, snort, and show the whites of the eyes. By the time the boy had set down the saddle and started over to the horse with his blanket, the gelding was throwing his head and pulling at the halter, simply terrified. It took me a minute to realize that the new blanket, bright-colored, flashy, and flapping in the breeze, was at least part of the problem. Besides that, it finally occurred to me, none of his equipment would look right to a horse, or smell right. There was an unmistakable new-leather smell to it, but none of the good old horsey smell that goes along with an old comfortable saddle. To make matters even worse, the beautiful new saddle was of light-colored, natural-finish leather. The horse had never before seen a saddle that wasn't dark from a lot of use.

We set all the new tack aside, and to test our theory, I got an old blanket and saddle out of the pickup. Sure enough, after a look and smell or two, we could throw the old blanket across him, saddle and unsaddle, and the horse was perfectly content. Then it was a matter of convincing him that the new stuff was equally harmless.

It took an hour or so. We let him smell all the new tack. We rubbed his legs and body quietly with the new blanket, then let him smell it some more. I'll bet we saddled and unsaddled a couple of dozen times. We fed the horse a little grain while he still had the saddle on, and we outlined a program for follow up. For the next few weeks, whether he intended to ride or not, the boy would have the saddle near by when he'd feed the horse. Then it would be associated in the animal's mind with something pleasant. And by then the new tack would have some horse smell about it, rather than the scary new smell.

I've noticed this at other times. A horse just doesn't like new equipment. It has to get "broke in", like a pair of comfortable old boots, to be really acceptable.

I recently heard of a local cattleman who invested in a new saddle to the tune of about $650. Of course, you have to see if it's going to fit the horse's withers properly, so he got out his old cow horse, Cochise, to try it on. He tied the horse to the ladder going up into the barn loft, and swung the new saddle up onto the animal's back. It smelled funny and sounded odd, with the squeak of new leather and the rustle of the protective plastic cover still over the seat and cantle.

All hell broke loose. By the time the fracas was over, the horse had "nearly pulled down the barn", wrecked the ladder, and thrown a real bucking fit. The $650 saddle was kicked over in the dirt by the fence. This is not a green-broke colt, you understand, but a steady old cow horse. His owner was astonished.

"Who'd have thought," he wondered, "that he'd act like that

over a new saddle!"

"Well," answered his friend who had just witnessed the entire fiasco, "you got to remember, ol' Cochise never had nothin' new before."

Mom's Horse

I was afraid the mare's eyes were failing. In fact, one day last fall, I watched her turn in short circles in the pasture, and she seemed unable to see at all. I went out with the trailer next day, intending to take her to the vet. Oddly enough, she could see well enough so that I couldn't catch her. I had to give up the effort.

This mare isn't really old, only about ten or eleven. She has been one of our show animals, a favorite of my wife's. In fact, Edna bought the animal in the first place. We were looking at foals in the pasture of friends who were pretty big horse breeders at the time. They priced this filly too low, and instantly Eddie spoke up.

"I'll take 'er!"

This, you understand, from my conservative little wife, who always said we had too many horses already.

So this has always been "Mom's horse." The mare grew out well, was trained to saddle at the appropriate age. One of our daughters rode her in competition, including the Miss Rodeo Kansas contest, and usually placed well. The one foal the mare has produced is a filly of excellent quality. We had bred for another foal this spring, but apparently missed.

And now the little mare was going blind, I was afraid. My worst fears were realized one afternoon when a neighbor phoned. Their house overlooks our north pasture, where we had half a dozen horses for the winter. One was Mom's mare.

There's a horse in trouble, the neighbor said. It seems to be down, tangled in the fence, and struggling. They could see this with binoculars, but couldn't tell much else.

I was at work, so Connie and Edna drove out, and I followed as soon as I could get away. The mare had apparently panicked, and it looked as though she had hit the fence at a full gallop. Steel posts were twisted up like corkscrews, and a good five-wire fence pretty well demolished. Connie had cut the mare out of the wire when I got there, and had her on her feet, cut and bleeding, but basically intact. I went home for the trailer and took the animal to the vet hospital. The next morning, of course, was spent fixing fence.

The verdict was depressing. The injuries from the fence would heal, but the mare was completely blind from cataracts. A hopeless situation in a horse.

Some horses can adapt to blindness, and will feel their way along with caution. This mare had demonstrated her inability to cope with it. She just isn't the proper temperament. She'd be a good brood mare, could probably raise some fine foals, but would need special care. Daily care, and a small enclosure or stall to live in, where she couldn't get in trouble by becoming disoriented. Someone would have to assume the job, or — I didn't like to consider the alternative.

We called a few friends with the sort of contacts we needed, and put out feelers. No luck. A lot of people were interested and sympathetic, but still, we could find no one who was prepared to take the job of caring for an otherwise helpless mare.

Finally, I had an inspiration. I recalled a family who had once asked about a horse. They had teenagers, a few acres in the country, they liked horses, had wanted to raise a foal. I called them.

I hope the story has as happy an ending as it looks right now. We'll breed the mare and these kids will be able to raise what should be a top quality foal or two (or more).

They can raise the foal they've wanted, the mare can be well cared for, and best of all, she can be useful, instead of being destroyed.

The Mothering Urge

Among females of almost any mammalian species, there is an extremely strong mothering urge. About the first time I remember this being called to my attention was when I was a kid.

A neighbor of my uncle's had accidentally run a mower bar over a nest of tiny baby rabbits while he was mowing hay. He felt sort of bad about it, and for no good reason put a couple of the survivors in his shirt pocket as he started back toward the house. Then he got to feeling pretty foolish, and wondered why he brought them in. He decided to just feed them to the old Tabby cat at the barn, who had a new litter of kittens. Then, all problems solved for the day, he went in to supper.

A few days later, he made a startling discovery. The old mama cat hadn't eaten the rabbits but *adopted* them. They grew up with the kittens in the barn, and eventually struck out on their own.

I have since heard of cats raising baby squirrels, possums, and once, a skunk. Apparently a mother cat is really a mothering being.

One time we had two mama cats who pooled their litters. They simply put all kittens of both batches together. Either cat would nurse any kitten, while the other cat would go out to hunt, and then they'd trade off. I'm sure that the urge varies with individual cats, though. We've had some that were pretty poor mothers, as I recall.

The same is true of our mares. Some are great mothers, some just so-so. One big black mare of ours lost her first colt. He died at about four days old. I don't know whether that has anything to do with her attitude or not, but she'll babysit any colt that's around. When we used to have four or five foals a year, they'd all straggle along after her, returning to their own mothers only to eat. And sometimes we've seen her even furnish a snack for somebody else's foal. She's always "talking" softly to them when they're small.

By contrast, another of our mares won't even answer her own foal when he's lost, excited, in trouble, and crying for her. She just calmly continues grazing.

History and fiction are full of stories of human infants raised by wolves, apes, wild dogs, and so on. Apparently some have a basis of fact.

All this was brought to mind recently when an Oklahoma reader sent me a clipping from the *Tahlequah Pictorial Press*. It's a story about a local quarter horse named Ole Fox who raises calves. Fox's owners have a dairy operation, and there are always calves to teach to eat from a bottle and then wean on to the feedlot. Fox, now 32 years old, has raised about a hundred calves. They are simply put in with the old mare and follow her as if she were their mother.

Fox "gathers" the calves like a hen with chicks, and will herd them into the shed when it rains. If there's not enough room, it is said, the mare stands outside in the rain.

She has raised three foals of her own and apparently just really likes "mothering." She has been known to try to break down a fence to steal another mare's foal.

The old mare will even allow the calves to try to nurse from her. Of course this is a sort of useless project, since she has no milk. The calves soon realize that the food supply is elsewhere.

Fox goes through a bereavement period when her charges graduate to the feedlot. She runs and calls frantically for a while, like any mare at weaning time. One thing will cure her separation blues, though . . . a new batch of calves to mother.

The Escapees

Horsin' Around Again

For some reason or other, spring is usually the time of year we have more trouble with horses and fences. Maybe it's that the fences aren't in top condition after a long winter. Maybe the horses are just a little green-starved and the grass looks greener you-know-where. At any rate, things get pretty exciting sometimes.

Like a couple of weeks ago when I got a frantic call that our stallion was loose. Most likely "Bubba" had been leaning over the fence to eat new sprigs of grass. The ground was soft after spring rains, and the steel posts just sort of laid down as he leaned. What was really a pretty good five-wire fence was suddenly something the horse could walk across, and he was loose.

Now when a stallion finds himself loose he seems obliged to do two things: 1) convince everybody that he's the greatest stud-horse in the world, and 2) see how destructive he can be. He accomplishes the former by screaming and racing around, rearing and striking across the fence at other animals. This in turn leads to the destructive phase of the operation.

At any rate, when I got home, our usually calm stallion was pretty psyched up. He was working hard on phase 2, and had already destroyed a couple of ten-foot sections of cedar rail fence. A few more good lunges and he'd have been out in the main part of the pasture with an assortment of young horses, including several of his daughters. (Not recommended.)

My wife was standing in the driveway in her wool cap and down jacket. She had a broken axe handle in her hand, and looked a bit irate. I wasn't sure whether the axe handle was intended for me or the stud-horse, but I didn't want to find out.

I got a bucket of grain and Bubba immediately became more interested in food than whatever else he'd had in mind. I put a rope on him and tied him to the hitch rail to cool off. Thus we were both spared the axe handle while I fixed the fence. Pretty soon he was his usual calm self, and so was my wife.

Then there was the excitement this morning, of a different

sort. A cross-fence was down in the pasture and horses where we didn't want them. Just nuisance stuff. At breakfast, Connie admitted she *might* not have turned the electric fence back on after throwing hay. I made some sarcastic remarks about not working if it's not on and went out to check it.

Sure enough, the hot wire was down, along with a tangle of stock panels and a busted wire gate. I was sorting all this out and attempting to restore order when I made a rather startling discovery. Apparently Connie *had* turned the electric fence back on after all. When I grabbed the wire, I got a shock that rattled my eyeteeth. For once, just for a minute there, I thought maybe that kid's just a little *too* dependable.

A Boy and a Horse

This is a true story, of local origin. I won't use the boy's name. Everyone who matters to him will know who he is, and I don't want to embarrass him by making his story any more public than that. Besides, he doesn't know I'm writing this.

For the past couple of years, folks driving past the Fairgrounds after school or on a weekend might often see a big gray horse. He was one of several horses boarded there by special arrangement with the Fair Board. And usually this horse was being worked, groomed, fed, or ridden, by a lanky teenager.

The story begins when the boy was about ten. His dad, a horse trainer and farrier, had several mares, and, in the course of things, raised a few foals. That year, one was a big iron-gray colt, sired by a well-known race horse in our area. The big gelding was a lanky thoroughbred type. He broke out well, and at the age of two started on the race track circuit. Now in fiction, Gray would have won the All-American Futurity and paid off the mortgage on the farm, but this was real life. The colt never quite hit the top. He was good, but so were a lot of other colts.

41

So, though he ran well, it became apparent that Gray wasn't going to be able to continue the racing game. All that travel, training, and entry fees become expensive, even for a horse that is *almost* a consistent winner.

At about this time the boy, who had always been nuts about horses, enrolled in the horse project in 4-H. He needed a horse to work with, and in spite of all the horses constantly around his dad's place, they were actually pretty limited in available horses for his project. He was finally given Gray to work with.

A worse possibility for a kid's 4-H horse would be hard to imagine — a race horse, just off the track, high-strung and of nervous temperament. And *big*. The animal towered over his young trainer. Besides, he had the lean greyhound build of a race horse, not the heavy-muscled massiveness so loved by judges in the stock horse classes at the fairs.

The team of boy and horse did have a couple of things going for them, however. This wasn't really a "first horse" for the boy. *His* first, maybe, but he'd been around horses all his life. The horse looked disproportionately big for the boy at first, but the kid was growing. As he took on his adolescent growth spurt, he began to catch up to the big gelding. Before long his lanky form was more appropriate to his lanky horse.

But the main thing going for the pair was hard work. The boy spent hours with the horse, patiently teaching a whole new set of skills. Walk, trot, canter, stop, back, right and left lead changes. It must have been confusing to the young race horse.

The first few tries at competition were disappointing, but then something began to happen. Judges began to notice the kid with the gray horse and they began to win. Not always in first place, but even under judges who liked other types of horses they were near the top. Horse and rider developed a smooth skill that became hard to beat. They were a real eye-catching pair.

This year, their third season together, Gray and the boy had placed well at the Lyon County Fair. They had qualified to attend the State Fair competition and were winding down a pretty successful season, when one afternoon Gray took suddenly ill. The veterinarian came out, treated and advised, and then returned several times at hourly intervals. But the effort was useless. In a few hours Gray was dead, from a twisted intestine.

As soon as I heard, I drove over to express my sympathy to my young friend. He was working with a yearling colt, but stopped to tell me the details of his loss.

"Well," I remarked, "That's a pretty good looking colt you have there."

"Yeah," the young man agreed sadly. "But he'll never be as good as Gray. And we should have had another 15 years."

I'd bet, though, on his ability to take another horse and get everything out of it that the horse has to give.

One More Winter

Her registered name is "WM's Olive Oyl." She's our oldest mare, the family's long-standing joke on Dad, and the worst-looking horse we ever had.

We bought Olive when she was about nine, as part of a four-horse package deal. She was heavy in foal to a national performance champion. When it got right down to it, what I was doing all the horsetrading for was that I wanted the unborn foal that Olive was carrying.

That filly later became one of our best performance horses. Even before the foal was born, however, I started to get the horselaugh from family and friends. You see, Olive is a "problem" horse. She has a chronic intestinal problem, lifelong, which causes constant diarrhea. It's worse when she's nervous. She requires extra care, special feed, and is just generally more bother than most.

Olive has a special personality, too. She's aggressive and even a little dangerous when she has a new foal. For just a few days, she'll bite and strike. But on the other hand, she allowed me to rescue her newborn foal from the flooding creek bank one year. I had to turn my back to her and pick up the foal in my arms. Olive could have injured me badly, but didn't. Only the year before she had bitten me hard enough to draw blood, just for looking at her new baby! Most of the year she's gentle as a lamb, though.

I guess Olive and I have come to understand each other. Probably this started when I got a little defensive about being laughed at over her. Sure, she's not very pretty. She's never been fat in her life, because of her digestive problem. She's always looked so poor I've hoped she'd be behind the barn when anybody came to look at horses.

But she has superior foals. I think we have received more actual income from sale of Olive's offspring than from any other animal. She's had fifteen altogether, not bad for a "problem" mare. One, before we owned her, was a national halter champion. Another is the only animal ever to win the 4-H performance trophy at our fair *twice*. She has others all around the country, working successfully at their jobs or making kids happy.

Last fall, after her fifteenth foal was weaned, I felt that Olive had earned retirement. She's coming 22, and I had in mind a year or two for her where she could just stand in the sun and eat grass with no responsibilities. We took her up to winter pasture.

A few weeks later, when I went to check on her, she was looking much worse. She had lost weight, seemed weak and staggering. I watched her a little while and noticed her grazing, then tossing her head and spitting out shreds of chewed bromegrass. Aha! A bad tooth, maybe. I brought the trailer and took her home to the barn.

In spite of special feed and shelter, Olive continued to lose weight. Her diarrhea became worse. Finally one cold night I came home and Connie told me the bad news.

"Dad, Olive can't get up."

Olive was lying down in the stall and wouldn't try to lift her head. She was shivering. Her coat was wet and plastered with mud, sweat, and manure. Her bedding was disarranged from repeated efforts to rise. I knew she'd never get up again. Well, old lady, I thought, you've been pretty good to us. I'll try to make you comfortable these last few hours.

I got her a bucket of warm water, and helped her hold her head up to drink. I fed her a few handfuls of her special ground feed, from my cupped hands. Then, over the next hour, I talked to her, encouraged her, and finally, with Olive and I both heaving, she actually tottered up and stood swaying on her feet again.

I suppose it would have been economically smart to put the poor old lady to sleep, but it's become a sort of challenge, now. Olive's picking up weight, a little bit. I brought her out today and groomed the mud out of her hair. She even tried to bite me a couple of times when I got too rough with the currycomb. She looks a lot better. Not good, but then she's never looked good. As I write, the dignified old mare is cropping grass on the front lawn, enjoying the sunshine. I'll go put her back in the barn pretty soon.

I think she'll make it through another year, now. I really think she understood what happened that cold night in January when she *almost* didn't get up again. You see, Olive and I sort of understand each other.

Horse People

Suicidal Tendencies

One weekend in May, we were scheduled to participate in a two-day horse show about a hundred miles away. I felt we were about as ill-equipped for this show as we've ever been. There just hadn't been time to get the animals ready. Of course, Connie had worked hard with her performance mare. My main concern was Betsy, a young filly we wanted to show. Betsy was only a few weeks old, had never been in a trailer before, and wasn't experienced in being around other horses. She was likely to be unpredictable. Besides, taking a young foal requires taking along her mama, too.

We attached the big trailer to our wheezing old pickup truck. Connie's mare would ride in one of the front stalls. Betsy and her mother were side by side in the rear. We were off.

About ten miles down the road, the steering wheel began to vibrate a little. I was about to pull over to investigate when a car passed us, frantically gesturing and pointing to the trailer. We had a flat tire.

The road shoulder wasn't very wide, but we got over, sort of. Worse, the shoulder was soft, and worse still, I couldn't find the jack handle. (It turned up at home, later.) I was standing there, wondering how to change a tire with no tools but a lug wrench, a hay hook, and a jack without a handle. I didn't want to unload inexperienced animals on the busy highway, so we really needed to do something without unloading a ton of horses if we could.

About this time salvation arrived in the form of some friends from down the road. Bob and Ann Doudican pulled up behind us and stopped. I knew they were heading for the same horse show, but I'd thought they were ahead of us. They had a jack, but it didn't fit under the trailer. They did have a scoop shovel, though. We blocked the axle up with rocks and then dug a hole under the flat tire with the hay hook and the scoop shovel. Finally we were on our way, an hour late.

Next we took a wrong turn and got lost. More time spent backtracking. We finally found the right town and asked directions to the arena. I was sure by this time we'd missed the baby colt classes, since I knew they were first, and we were later and later.

We overshot the turnoff to the arena because a tree had grown out over the sign. By the time we shot past and recognized our mistake, there was no place to turn the long trailer around. On down the highway about a half mile was a farmhouse. Maybe we could turn in their driveway. I hurriedly pulled in, backed around, and didn't notice that on the other side of the highway the ditch dropped off sharply. The wheels of the trailer slipped off the shoulder and the weight of the big mare in the back began to tilt the trailer, pulling the truck backwards with tires sliding and spinning. I set the brakes and leaped out to see how bad it was.

The trailer was tilted at about 45 degrees on its side and the big mare was down. I was frantically clawing open the back trailer gates to get to the animals when help arrived again in the form of Doudicans. They had overshot the turn, too, and spotted us in trouble. They couldn't fail to spot us. Traffic was blocked for a quarter mile both ways.

Bob and I pried open the damaged door and somehow managed to get the mare on her feet and out. She's a pretty easy-going old lady, so she started calmly eating grass. With part of the weight out, we were able to drive forward and pull the trailer up and out of the ditch.

We arrived with hardly a scratch. The show had started late, so we did get Betsy in the ring, where she placed third in her class. Connie and her mare placed well, too, but it was sure a harrowing day.

As Ann Doudican said that evening, people who show horses have to have suicidal tendencies.

Horse People

Rosie

A few years ago we had an unusual boarder. We were renting pasture for a couple of horses to a graduate student at the college. Through a mixup in communications, she came up without an apartment lease she thought she had, and the result was a real problem about a place to live.

We had an extra bedroom. Since Rosie was out at our place every day with her horses anyway, it just seemed logical to rent her the room. That was our introduction to a most unusual person, who soon became "family." She pitched in with chores from the first. Better than some members of the family, I'll have to admit. Not household chores, you understand. Farm chores. Rosie could buck hay bales with most men.

She was excellent with livestock, and our kids immediately began to learn a lot about horsemanship from our boarder. Our oldest daughter went with Rosie to compete in a couple of horse shows. Our youngest, two years old, spent a lot of happy hours riding one of Rosie's horses. They'd snub a halter rope to Rosie's saddle horn, and Connie would proudly ride down the road holding her own reins. She learned a lot that year.

Rosie's most unusual attribute was probably her means of working her way through school. This young woman actually financed part of her master's degree in education by shoeing horses. She's an excellent farrier, too. Very good with problem feet. She was once pictured in *Western Horseman* magazine, fitting shoes to the mounts of a couple of cross-country riders from New York.

Even more special than her ability with horses is Rosie's kindness and generosity with people. In her work with youngsters as a teacher, she has been more help to more troubled youngsters than anyone could tell. Strict, a tough disciplinarian, but fair, and respected by her students.

She came from a large ranch family in the Flint Hills, somewhere about the middle of the series of youngsters. When we attended her parents' Golden Wedding Anniversary, we heard a story that pretty well shows Rosie's place in the family. Her father had recently had eye surgery for cataracts. As the date for his hospitalization drew closer, the old rancher was obviously more nervous and concerned about it. Finally he called Rosie. Would she, he asked, come up to Topeka to be with him the day of his surgery? Of course — but why, Daddy, when there are several of the kids right near there who'd be happy to be with you?

"Well," he replied hesitantly with a catch in his voice, "it's always seemed to me like you treat your horses purty good."

Shortly after she left our fireside, Rosie married a cattleman she met on the horse show circuit. The marriage ended tragically a few years later when her husband died of cancer. She continued to teach, run the ranch, and raise horses — registered Arabians now. Summers are spent ranching, horse showing, and doing custom hay work.

Not long ago Rosie had a fall from a young horse she was working. Her back was sprained a bit, and she missed several days of school. My wife drove up to see how she was getting along. Rosie was still crippling around, not back to work yet. But she was concerned. She had tickets for a bus trip to the National Finals Rodeo, and wasn't sure she'd be able to make the trip.

I laughed when Edna came home and told me about it. Rosie would *crawl* to Oklahoma City, I predicted, if she had to, to use those Rodeo tickets. The following weekend we saw her at the National Finals Rodeo. Stiff and sore, you understand, but still in there pitching! And treating her horses pretty good.

An English Saddle on the Prairie?

One of the exciting occurrences around the old home town in 1977 was the filming of the TV movie, "Mary White."

Mary was the daughter of the famous journalist, William Allen White, editor of the Emporia Gazette. She was killed in 1921, at age 16, when she was knocked from her horse by a tree limb. A movie which encompasses the last two years of Mary White's life was later shown on ABC, starring Kathleen Beller as Mary.

There were a number of things of interest to horsemen in the filming of the movie here in Emporia. Of course, "Hollywood horses" were imported for the film. A Hollywood horse doesn't necessarily come from Hollywood, but is a professional movie horse. They must be able to ignore all the lights, reflectors, snaky-looking electric cables, and whirring cameras, and be ready to move out on cue. They are real troupers.

In this case, two identically marked animals were used to play Mary's horse, "Red", apparently to alternate in case one became bored or tired. Both were nice sorrel geldings with white stockings and a narrow blaze. One interesting thing amused some of the observers. While one horse was "on camera", his stand-in back at the trailer would call and whinny constantly. I guess even Hollywood horses aren't immune to becoming herd-bound for their friends.

The fall from the horse in the accident scene was filmed using the producer's daughter as a stunt girl. Arionna Radnitz, who resembles Kathleen Beller considerably anyway, is a superb horsewoman, and helped with the horseback scenes. Actually, footage was taken with both girls taking the fall, and what we later saw on film was probably a composite version, with clips from several cameras.

In the movie, the accident was shown at a canter. Actually, it occurred at a walk. Mary was brushed off by a tree branch while looking back to wave at a friend, and struck her head on a stone curb. I suppose we can allow a little leeway. Poetic license, I guess. It makes a better picture at a canter.

Great effort was made to research the type of clothing, cars, and styles of the 1920's. Mary's clothing was probably unique riding garb, even for the time. Old pictures show her wearing a World War I army-style hat — the flat-brimmed, pointed-top

Horsin' Around Again

campaign hat like Smoky Bear's. Kathleen Beller sure does look good in one.

One question was a brief problem. What sort of saddle did Mary White use? There was a rumor around town for a day or two that they intended to use a sidesaddle. That idea was met with snorts of scorn by horse-oriented Emporians. That would be decades out of date. Next, the rumor factory produced the information that Mary would ride English style. This produced more snorts of scorn. I personally thought that she would have been riding on an old-fashioned high-back Western stock saddle.

As a matter of fact, I rather doubted that there was even a single English saddle in all of Lyon County in 1921. When I was growing up, all the cow-country people used to sort of snicker at anyone who tried riding English. Still do, to some extent. And as for the double English rein, this was always looked on in our part of the country as the height of stupidity.

"If you can't handle him with one set of reins, you sure ain't goin' to with two," was a sort of slogan of derision.

Actually, I doubt if the type of saddle and tack Mary White used was much of a problem to the producers of the movie. It was more of a topic for discussion among horse people of the area when they'd meet during the few weeks "Mary White" was being filmed.

I really stuck my neck out. I was so convinced that Mary would have been riding a stock saddle that I was loud in my opinion. I was talking when I should have been listening, as the saying goes, and consequently made a fool of myself.

Because somebody turned up with an old photograph of Mary White and her horse. And wonder of wonders, the girl actually rode an English saddle, with a Western bridle and a curb bit. Nothing conventional about Mary!

And when it got right down to it, what they actually used for filming was an English-style bareback saddle pad. Oh, well, close enough. It turned out to be a great movie, anyway.

Horse People

Dad

A number of readers knew my dad, or were aware that he passed away recently at the age of 86. Since that time, I have spent a lot of thought on the tremendous number of changes that he saw in his lifetime.

Born in 1888, he grew up in Joplin, Missouri, in a setting that was still pretty "frontier." The American public had barely gotten over the shock of the Custer fiasco at the Little Big Horn, and there were, of course, no cars, planes, radio, TV, or even electricity, except as an interesting experiment. All transportation was by horse, train, or on foot.

One of young Charlie Coldsmith's first regular jobs was to drive the local milk cows out of town to graze every morning and bring them back to town at milking time. This was an easy job, because each cow knew her own barn, and all he had to do was head the herd into the dirt-paved street in the late afternoon. Every cow would turn aside when she passed her own place, to be milked and spend the night in the barn.

Long hours were available to the barefoot young cowherder to lie on the grass and watch the clouds, or swim in the creek, or watch wild turkeys. Once he even found a turkey's nest, and the eggs made an addition to the family's usually thin larder.

Somehow, at a very early age, the boy was influenced strongly by a Methodist Sunday school teacher, and he decided he should enter the ministry. He must have taken a lot of ridicule. No one the family knew had ever attended college, and most had never finished high school. But Dad worked his way through college, a graduate degree in theology, and was ultimately awarded a Doctor of Divinity degree, perhaps his most cherished accomplishment. He became well known in Methodist circles, twice serving in an administrative capacity as District Superintendent.

Charlie married a pretty redhead whom he met at college, and they raised four children, all of whom have brought them a certain degree of pride. She preceded him in death by a few years.

I never heard my father swear, despite his boyhood in the rough end of Joplin. His strongest expletive was "Oh, pshaw!" However, he did understand proper use of strong language. I once overheard him talking to my sister about a suitor who wished to marry her. I didn't think much of this dude. He was too prissy. Apparently my dad felt similarly about it. "Honey," I heard him tell her, "he's a nice boy, but I'd feel a lot better about him if he'd just once get up enough nerve to say 'damn'!"

He raised irises, producing several varieties that have become commercial. The last spring of his life, at 85, he was hybridizing flowers to produce seed that he knew would not bloom for two more years.

He retired from full-time ministry in 1954, but asked to be assigned a part-time church. Charlie didn't know how to do anything part time, however, and plunged into the ministry of a struggling small church with the same intensity he had always used. The dying little church began to prosper, and he served it well until the time of his death. Charlie did not believe in retirement. He had preached an excellent sermon five days before his death by a heart attack, and the previous day was reading, researching, and writing new material.

We received a letter last year in which he said he had to sign off and get it in the mail so he could go to the Golden Age Club. "Some of those old people aren't very interesting," he continued, "but somebody has to go over and cheer them up!"

That was my father. From a barefoot urchin with a hickory hat, in a frontier town, to a respected theologian who was interested in everything, and watched men land on the moon via the TV in his living room, he felt that he had a fascinating life.

One of his church members summed up the manner of his death. "I think he and God just talked it over and decided it was time for Charlie to retire."

Horse People

The Elder Statesman

One of my favorite horsemen is Alfred M. Landon, who at eighty-nine still rode his horse a few miles almost daily.

Landon was again catapulted into the national spotlight as one of the introductory speakers at the Republican National Convention of 1976. He emerged with the image of elder statesman of the party. His views were listened to and respected even by the network media representatives, who usually don't listen to or respect anybody. This man gives the impression of a wise, alert statesman with a relaxed good humor and a keen interest in everything.

During the presidential campaign in 1936 I remember wearing "Landon for President" buttons with sunflowers on my beanie cap. I was a real admirer of our governor, and proud of the fact that a Kansan had been selected to run for the highest office in the land. I was a little bewildered over the election debacle. *I* knew how great a man Governor Landon was. How could so many people fail to see this and be so wrong in their voting? (Occasionally I still feel this way after elections.)

At any rate, Franklin Roosevelt stayed in the White House, and Alf Landon stayed in Topeka. He and Mrs. Landon settled down comfortably in their colonial-style country home, where the former governor could write, carry on his business activities, and enjoy his extensive library and his horses.

Landon was already a respected statesman, of course. He had become known as a leader in the growing petroleum industry, with foresight and financial ability. As two-term Governor of Kansas in the early thirties, he was notable for a stable state economy and a balanced state budget, a rarity even then.

Although retired as a public office-seeker after the 1936 campaign, Landon continued his interest in national, state, and local affairs. In fact, his wide range of interests is probably one of the factors that has kept him young. Another is physical activity. Nearly every day, the vigorous former governor walks or jogs a bit, and then takes a ride on his sorrel gelding. Governor

57

Landon has always admired good horses, and has ridden for most of his life. (How many men of 89 do you know who ride horseback almost daily?)

He was unable to celebrate his 89th birthday on September 9th with his customary ride, however. He was busy elsewhere. A recognition celebration at Kansas State University had been planned to honor the elder statesman, so the big red horse stayed in the barn.

It was my privilege as a young YMCA youth worker in Topeka in the early 1950's to meet Alf Landon on a number of occasions. I was always impressed by his warm, quiet demeanor, his perceptiveness, and above all, his quick sense of humor.

On one special occasion, I attended a banquet as a representative from the "Y." The occasion, I believe, was the 65th anniversary of the Salvation Army in Topeka. Dignitaries from throughout the state and even the nation were present. Various church groups and religious organizations were represented as the Army celebrated the anniversary. The master of ceremonies was Alfred M. Landon.

Entertainment for the evening was provided by the Chicago Staff Band of the Salvation Army. I have rarely heard so thrilling a concert. There is nothing like a Sousa-style brass band, but the high point of the concert was a bass drum solo. That's right! A retired officer put on a spectacular show with two drumbeaters, whirling them expertly on the straps. The sticks whirled over his head, across the top of the big drum, booming the message across the room. His performance brought a standing ovation.

Landon invited the elderly gentleman to the podium and interviewed him briefly. He was Commissioner Ernest Pugmire, formerly National Commander. A few years before, he had retired from active service in the Army; however, he had continued his role as bass drummer in this, probably the finest of Salvation Army bands. His bass drum career, he added, had started at the age of ten or eleven, when he played the drum in a Salvation Army street band. A minimum of mental arithmetic made it obvious that here was a man who had played the Salvation Army drum for well over a half century.

"Now that," observed Landon, the famous twinkle in his eyes, "is what I call playin' the drum to beat Hell!"

Note: As this book goes to press, Alf Landon is still going strong at 94. According to Senator Bob Dole, Landon has almost stopped his daily ride, though. The horse, he explains, is getting too old.

Nuyaka

We had only one foal on the place last year. One of our best Appaloosa performance mares presented us with a big leggy colt, one of our best ever, I thought. His breeding was excellent, both his grandsires having been National Performance Champion in different years. Boy, I thought, if we'd only had bloodlines like this when we were more actively competing on the breed show circuit.

The colt grew well, was strong and straight and one of our smartest ever. He's the only colt I ever halter-broke that didn't have to throw himself at least once to learn not to pull back on the rope.

We named him "Nuyaka", a Creek Indian name from Edna's old stompin' ground in Oklahoma. The Appaloosa is actually more appropriate to Nez Perce history, but that's pretty variable any more. We'd been saving the name Nuyaka for a special foal, and this one was it.

As a coming yearling, he looks even better. He's a rich bay, with splashes of white across the hips, and a classic sort of head. We were talking about putting him in training early, and trying to find someone who'd really campaign him. If this colt doesn't do well, it's just our fault, I figured.

Then one evening we received a phone call from a friend

who's a professor at the Haskell Indian Junior College at Lawrence. They were preparing to inaugurate a new president, he told me. He would be Gerald E. Gipp, a Sioux, the first president who was actually a Native American himself.

To mark the occasion, a dance and celebration would be held in his honor. As a symbolic gesture, they wished to give him a gift, and the traditional gift for such an occasion would be a horse. They had collected donations, and were looking for a suitable animal.

Well, the figure he mentioned was pretty low. About dog food price, actually. They knew this, he told me. He had called me, knowing my horse interests, and hoping I'd know someone who had a weanling or *some* sort of animal to carry out the symbolism involved. They had a trainer who could handle the horse if they could find one for the amount they could afford.

I promised to ask around and hung up to explain to Edna. I was pretty pessimistic. As I sat there, I kept thinking about Nuyaka. He'd be perfect for the purpose, but was worth easily three times their available funds.

Finally it was Eddie who spoke up. "Honey, couldn't we let them have Nuyaka for the money they have, and we'll donate the difference?"

Bless her heart, she wanted to help them as bad as I did. We called our friend back.

He and the trainer showed up a couple of days later, with a trailer in tow. The trainer was a young man with a better touch with a horse than I ever saw. He and Nuyaka hit it off immediately. We completed the paperwork, and they headed back up the turnpike toward Lawrence.

I felt good about the whole thing. Here was an outstanding colt, a Nez Perce horse with a Creek name, raised by a couple of palefaces. He was being transported to Lawrence by a PhD college professor who is a Delaware with a Kiowa wife, will be trained by a Cherokee and presented to a college president who is a Sioux. That really combines a lot of tradition, and is actually what it's all about, I guess.

I hope the symbolic presentation went well, and I hope that the people involved at that end of the transaction feel as honored to be a part of it as we do.

Dudes and Tenderfeet

Dorothy Johnson, author of *The Man Who Shot Liberty Valance* and other western favorites, makes an interesting distinction between terms. "Dude" and "tenderfoot", she says, are often used interchangeably, but this is completely inaccurate.

Both terms were applied to a newcomer to the west, but with considerable difference in connotation. A "dude" was a sort of derogatory term. This was a fellow from the east who didn't understand the west, but didn't like it or anything about it, and fought every minute of it. He was a misfit, and was accorded no respect by the westerner. He'd never make it.

On the other hand, there was another breed of easterner on the frontier — the "tenderfoot." This was the easterner who came west and tried to acclimatize. He loved the country, rough thought it might be. He was ready to learn by trial and error, and to take his lumps when he made a mistake. He might be ridiculed by the westerner, and might be subjected to a lot of practical jokes and good-natured hazing. But by and large, he had a certain amount of respect going for him because he was trying to make it in the west. If he did succeed, he'd be welcome to the fold.

I saw this distinction in action recently. The Western Writers group had, as part of their conference program, an evening at a place called Indian Cliffs. We were taken by bus about thirty miles into the desert outside El Paso. There we loaded on horses or on hay wagons pulled by horse teams to go on out to the Cliffs, another three or four miles into the desert. This was the best

Horsin' Around Again

kind of an old-fashioned hay ride, with a pretty good guitar player "riding shotgun" and singing.

It was pretty hot that evening, probably still about 90 degrees, and I noticed one very uncomfortable young man. He was a publisher's representative from New York and looked like he'd never been on this sort of evening before. He was wearing a nice-looking tweedy sport coat and a tie. When I first noticed him, he was sitting on the edge of the hay rack, sweat dripping from the end of his nose. I never saw a person look more miserable. He's not going to make it, I thought. He'll be telling all his New York friends about the miserable time he had Out West.

However, it wasn't long until he'd shed the coat and tie, and looked a little better. Shortly after we got to the cliffs a pretty rough little sandstorm blew in, and everybody was sort of spitting sand and making remarks about "true grit." I thought about the New Yorker and wondered how he was doing, but didn't see him just then.

The storm was pretty well over by the time they served dinner. A great meal, with a two-pound charcoal-broiled steak, Mexican-style beans with chile gravy, cole slaw, and big hunks of homemade bread. Our easterner was packing it in pretty well, so I figured his evening wasn't a total loss.

Then the group loosely assembled around a campfire, with a huge enameled coffeepot going, and the guitar player tuned up again. He could handle most any request, and the singing went on until well after dark.

As we climbed back on the hay racks to head home in the moonlight, I happened to run into the New Yorker again. His jacket was slung carelessly over his shoulder now, and he was obviously having a great time.

"Do you do things like this in Kansas?" he asked me. I assured him that such things do happen sometimes.

"Wow!" he murmured. "This is fantastic. I didn't even know people lived like this!"

Maybe I was wrong about this kid, I thought. I think he's going to make it.

Horse People

The Trophy We Don't Have

Back more years than I like to think about, we hauled a horse quite a distance to participate in a big youth show. We were pretty new to competition showing, and although our daughter April and her horse were looking pretty good, they hadn't really started to win much yet. They were working hard at it, though, and I hoped she'd show up satisfactorily in this kind of major competition.

I felt that of the several events they entered, their best possibility was in the Horsemanship class, age twelve and under. There were over twenty riders in the class, and as the judge spotted little mistakes, he began to weed out the kids who weren't going to place. These were sent down to one end of the arena to wait, while those still in the competition continued to work. I thought he liked the way April worked, because he kept watching her.

Finally, there were only six or eight riders still competing in the center of the arena. The judge brought them into line, had each back a few steps or some similar maneuver to make his final decisions. He scribbled the winning numbers on his card, handed it to the ring steward, and left the arena for lunch break. There was the usual interminable waiting while the ring steward walked over to hand in the results at the announcers' stand. Then all the numbers had to be matched to names on the roster, and at last the announcer began.

"In fifth place, Number 78, Jimmy Blake."

We held our breaths, waiting for "Number 53, April Coldsmith." The announcer continued to call off names and numbers, and our girl sat straight and tall in the arena. When she wasn't second, I almost jumped up to holler. I knew she'd turned in a flawless performance, and there was now no question but that the judge knew it, too.

". . . and in first place," the announcer chanted, while we nearly exploded, "is Number 58, Miss Sally Jane Smith!"

There was a delighted shriek of disbelief from a family up

in the stands behind us. A little girl with tears of joy in her eyes urged her fat little horse forward to receive her trophy. Forward from the *far end* of the arena, from the group long ago eliminated from the competition. I realized what had happened. Somewhere between the judge's scribbled note card and the confusion in the announcer's booth, somebody had read a 53 as a 58. Thoughts raced through my mind as I ran down to the arena gate to meet a disappointed April.

How should we protest? Where, when, and to whom? The judge had already gone to lunch, and the announcer and his helpers were leaving.

April was calm and dry-eyed. I walked along beside her horse, and we hadn't gone but a few steps before we passed a happy family scene. A proud young couple and a couple of kids were all talking at once, crying with joy, and hugging, alternately, Sally Jane Smith, the fat little mare, and a tall silver trophy.

"Daddy," said April calmly, not even slowing her horse, "that little girl has my trophy, doesn't she?"

"Yes, honey," I gulped, past the big lump in my throat, "she sure does."

Now, how could we have broken up a scene like that? We didn't protest, and in the confusion, apparently no one else noticed the error. At least, nobody said anything.

April knew she'd won. We knew it. Why rock the boat? We didn't want to sound like poor losers.

And yet, if I had it to do over, I wonder. What would I do?

Horse People

Charlie Crouse

One of the things I enjoy about visiting a different part of the country is that it's an opportunity to hear some new stories. Every community in the world has its own assortment of legends and local tales. This is especially true of smaller, more rural communities. The local history, especially the interesting, fun part of it, is handed down by word of mouth. We're losing a lot of this charm by our trend to a highly mobile population, I'm afraid, but that's another story.

I learned about Charlie Crouse not long ago. Crouse is a real character, an early rancher on the Green River. I've seen the remains of his corrals and outbuildings. Crouse Canyon near the Colorado-Wyoming border is named after him. But Crouse is also a character of another sort. On his own from the age of nine, he made his way on the rough frontier in any way he could. He acquired a wife and a partner, and started ranching. Charlie had a good eye for horseflesh, and raised some superior race horses, described glowingly in contemporary accounts.

Crouse was also a very colorful individual. He had two sons, and it was said he never referred to either of them by name. One was customarily called "that red-headed S.O.B." and even more colorful language was reserved for the dark-haired Crouse offspring.

One story about Crouse stands out among all the rest. In the area of Green River City there was a well-known race horse called Tom Thumb. Crouse and his partner matched a good young mare against him and were beaten. Even more irritating than the financial loss was the constant ridicule by one of the winners of a side bet with Crouse, a tavern owner named McIntosh. Crouse became increasingly rankled by the taunts, but bided his time, pretending nothing was amiss. Eventually, he made a trip to Missouri, and in the course of the journey acquired a horse. The promising thoroughbred, already a proven winner as a three-year-old, was quietly brought back to the ranch on the Green and placed in intensive race training.

Meanwhile, the appearance of the horse was allowed to deteriorate. He was not groomed, his mane and tail were allowed to grow shaggy, and thistles were artfully placed in his forelock. With feet long and untrimmed, and in winter coat, the horse became the most disreputable-looking animal ever seen in the area. Crouse then took the horse to Green River City with a string of other animals for sale. He was sold to a sheepherder as a pack horse for forty dollars.

The next part of the plan was a trip to McIntosh's saloon. Crouse, without much trouble, picked an argument with the saloonkeeper. An argument, naturally, about race horses. The climax came when Crouse, after defending the qualities of his roan mare, stated she had been sick that day, and anyway, Tom Thumb wasn't much of a horse.

"Hell," said Charlie Crouse, "I just sold a horse to a sheepherder for $40 that can run the legs off Tom Thumb!"

And he settled back to enjoy his drink. McIntosh quietly sent for the owner of Tom Thumb. They located the sheepherder, and examined the horse, which appeared to be just a big mustang, broke to pack. The sheepherder proved legitimate and unknown to Crouse prior to that day. For five dollars he allowed them to borrow the horse for a race, and the plotters gleefully returned to challenge Crouse.

Stories recount the size of "stacks of bags of $20 gold pieces," each man betting everything he owned. Side bets flourished.

It really wasn't much of a race. The sheepherder's horse beat the famous Tom Thumb by five lengths, and this on a half-mile track. McIntosh was deeply in debt to "almost everybody on the river."

After the race, Crouse bought the bay back from the sheepherder for $500. That stalwart individual went on his way, no doubt convinced that all gringos are crazy. Otherwise, *amigo*, why would a man sell a horse for $40, then the same man buy it back the same day for more than a year's wages?

Horse People

Grandpa

In the past few weeks a number of people we know have mentioned it: when am I going to write about being a grandfather?

I don't know why grandparents come in for so much teasing. It's no big deal. About like being father of the bride, only less so. I guess I figured I wasn't old enough to be anybody's grandfather, though.

My own grandfather, the only one I knew, must have been nearing seventy when I was born. I remember him as a kindly man, a little frail, with an endless supply of stories about the "Olden Days." He had homesteaded on the prairie, hunted buffalo, raised cattle and horses, and was an excellent carpenter and cabinetmaker.

He made toys, too, to delight the hearts of youngsters. Boats, pop guns, jumping jacks. Horses, cows, and other animals. And blocks. One bottom drawer in a dresser at Grandpa's was full of blocks, spools, and interesting pieces of wood. Not painted playroom blocks, you understand. Just wooden pieces he'd sawed off the end of a board and stuck in his pockets because they were nice shapes for kids to play with.

Sometimes if we were good, he'd get out an ostrich egg he'd brought back from a long-ago trip to Florida. It was kept carefully wrapped in cotton batting, in a shoe box. We didn't get to play with it, just look.

One of his biggest disappointments, I think, was when he no longer had the strength in his shoulders to throw the heavy harness up over the backs of the draft horses. His expertise was still highly regarded, though. I can remember the young farmers asking his advice on crops and horses and butchering a hog.

My kids will remember only one grandfather, too. My dad. He was a Methodist minister, who died a few years ago at 86, with a new sermon for the next Sunday partly finished on his desk. He had a sense of humor, and was a great gardener. They will remember him playing the harmonica, and watching them ride the horses, and sitting in our kitchen drinking my wife's good coffee.

And now, suddenly, we are somebody's grandparents. It's an awesome responsibility. I hope I can get the hang of it right off. I'm sure Edna intends to spoil the little feller. Probably I will, too. But we wouldn't except that he's obviously a very superior-type child. He looks a lot like his dad. Some of my kids were accused of that, too, as I recall.

He's got long bones and big feet and hands, so will probably be a tall man. The Coldsmith cleft or dimple shows in his chin. He is a pretty easygoing little feller, doesn't fuss much or loud, just seems interested in everything that's going on in this strange world's he's landed in. I like that. I think his great-grandfather and his great-great-grandfather would have approved, too.

Maybe he'll like to tramp around with me and I can take him fishing. Maybe this grandfather bit won't be so bad at all. Do I want him to be a horseman? That's up to him. Some of our own kids wanted to, some didn't, and I hope they always knew it was okay either way. I rather think if Nathan is interested, I know where he can find a horse to ride. His Aunt Connie has already figured out that her first little mare would be nice for a nephew to use.

Horse People

Tom Bass

He was born in 1859, to a slave girl in Boone County, Missouri. His father was the slave girl's white master. From these ignoble beginnings, Tom Bass rose to national renown, and became acquainted with five presidents.

At a very early age, young Tom showed a remarkable ability to communicate with animals, especially horses. The boy, newly freed from slave status, was working at a livery stable in Mexico, Missouri. It became apparent that the young negro was so adept at managing and training horses that local horsemen sought his advice with their problems. As word of Bass' expertise spread, horsemen from the entire area began to bring problem horses, or animals for special training. He opened his own training stable at Mexico, and married a young woman named Angia, in 1882. A son, Inman, was born to the couple, but died in childhood.

The fame of Tom Bass and his skill with horses spread. He invented new methods and equipment for use in training. The "Bass bit", a training bit used to avoid damage and discomfort to the mouth of a young animal, is still used by many trainers.

Bass was especially adept in two fields of equine endeavor. He could "high school" a horse with uncanny ability. Such horsemen as Buffalo Bill Cody called upon Tom Bass to train the trick and fancy mounts for his Wild West Show.

The other specialty was that of the formal show ring. Bass' training methods and his quiet, firm, yet dignified and gentlemanly manner lent themselves well to the world of dressage. Horsemen in show competition increasingly sought the young trainer's skill and advice in the handling of their mounts and preparation for the show ring.

Finally came a critical turning point in history. A horse owner, his animal ready for competition, realized that no one could achieve top performance from the mare except her trainer, Tom Bass. With many misgivings, the animal was entered in a competitive show in northern Missouri. Bass, born a slave, entered the elite world of the show ring in the clothing of a gentleman. This was the first time in America that a black man was to ride in a formal show arena. The horse performed well, and Tom Bass won the class. Far from being critical, as had been feared, the crowd loved it. Bass left the arena to a standing ovation.

From that time on, Bass was a familiar figure at equine events throughout the country. He remained intensely interested in the show arena. He is credited with organizing the first formal horse show in Kansas City, the forerunner of the famous American Royal.

At the height of his career, Tom Bass was invited to perform in England for Queen Victoria. He politely declined, stating that he had an unusual fear of the long sea voyage. He did perform before five presidents, and numbered among his friends and acquaintances many famous people. At the time of his death in 1934, his eulogy was written by another great horseman, his longtime friend, Will Rogers.

In October, 1977, a special ceremony was held at the Elmwood Cemetery at Mexico, Missouri. The occasion was the dedication of new markers over the graves of Tom and Angia Bass. Representatives of the Audrain County Historical Society and Saddle Horse Museum participated. The headstones are the gift of the American Royal Horse Show Association, in appreciation of the contribution of Tom Bass, a great horseman and a great American.

Horse People

The Lazy SOB

I had been working on the idea for an article — the thought that we're all longing for a return to a simpler set of values. Why not end the column, I thought, with the well-known poem, "Code of the Cow Country"? It expresses the idea I was trying for. I knew I'd need copyright permission, so I contacted the author, S. Omar Barker, obtaining his address through the Western Writers of America organization.

Right away, a reply came from Mr. Barker in New Mexico. When I first opened the envelope, there was a greeting card from the Leanin' Tree collection. It had a picture of a grizzled old cowboy on the front, and inside, Mr. Barker had typed a short message.

"I write verses for this outfit," he began, "and they keep me overstocked with cards, all for free. That's why I push 'em off inappropriately as to date."

The printed message in the card was a very western verse by S. Omar Barker, and ended in "Happy Birthday." It was signed in blue ink at the bottom, "For whenever." I chuckled and turned to the letter itself.

"Dear Mr. Coldsmith," it began, "Of course you are welcome to use 'Code of the Cow Country' in your column."* The rest of that paragraph dealt with details about the copyright and the poem, and then he plunged on into the interesting part of the letter.

"I'm only 83," he continued, "too young to have been there in the great trail-driving days, but in my youth I knew some who had been. . . . And I would bet my saddle against last week's cow track that most of them would rate the 'code' of my poem as accurate in the main."

He discussed a couple of thoughts about the poem, and slight trouble he had with the rhyme and rythm. The "little ol' verse", as he calls it, was written in 1929, "to sell to a Western pulp magazine for about ten bucks."

There followed a paragraph about a remark I had made in

---

*See "Code of the Cowboy," p. 107

my letter, referring to a time when "all the good guys wore white hats." This idea, of course, is pure Hollywood. As Mr. Barker says, "Stetsons were gray when new, and a dingy gray before long. But black hats were not uncommon on both good guys and bad."

There is a nostalgia for the old days, he feels, and for the reason I mentioned. Right and wrong were easier to sort out, for the simple reason that ". . . the moral principles of the times had not yet been all mixed up by so many pseudo philosophers generally called psychologists and psychiatrists. . . ."

"But never mind. Here I am at 83, a genuine paradox my-ownself: somewhat short of breath but still long-winded. Excuse it, please.

Regards and best wishes,
(Signed) S. Omar Barker,
The Lazy S O B"

Then the "lazy S O B" was written in blue ink as a brand (ᴎOB). As cow-country people know, any letter or number lying on its side in a brand is read as "lazy." Therefore "Lazy S O B."

I had never before thought of this pun on S. Omar Barker's initials. Then he added a postscript which is perhaps best of all.

"Actually my brand when I had a few cattle was Lazy SB (ᴎ B) because when I applied for Lazy SOB they told me some other SOB already had it."

Well, friends, I'd like to be able to think like that and write like that when I'm 83.

Or right now, for that matter.

The Folk Hero

I think I'd be guilty of gross negligence if, somewhere along the line, I didn't write something about John Wayne. With his death in 1979 America has lost one of her heroes. And we're sure getting short on heroes.

When I was a kid there were a lot of people in public life for kids to admire and try to pattern a life after. Now it's pretty thin. It's the popular thing to try to find the weakness in any leader. Somewhere along the line we have to realize that when we drag our potential heroes down, we drag down all of us to the same mediocre level. We have to have somebody to admire. And somebody who could be respected and admired for his straightforward consistency was John Wayne. Even people who disliked his politics admitted that here was a man to be respected. They always knew where he stood. No one ever questioned his love of his country. He was patriotic when patriotism was not in vogue.

His name was originally Marion Michael Morrison, born in Winterset, Iowa. In college at the University of Southern California, he was a fraternity man, played football, and graduated in 1929. When his name was changed by Hollywood, as was the custom in the 1930's, there was little to suggest that John Wayne would become a household word.

I don't need to tell anyone reading this about the type of roles he played. Wayne was one of the biggest box-office attractions of all time. His Academy Award was in 1970 for the role of the marshal in "True Grit." One of my friends once said that in salty old Rooster Cogburn, John Wayne finally got to play John Wayne. However, I always felt that every role he played was John Wayne. The critics sometimes were a bit hard on him, but the audiences loved him. As Jack Lemmon said at the time of Wayne's death, he ". . . was always bigger than life, but he never abused it."

His nickname, "Duke", has no romantic significance. It was the name of a pet dog when he was a kid.

By the time of the Korean War, a generation of Americans had grown up watching his movies. It came to be that in GI slang in Korea, an act of heroism was referred to as a "John Wayne."

Despite the rugged front, John Wayne's fellow workers knew him as a sentimentalist. ". . . A big generous heart and a great soul," said Buddy Ebsen.

At the time of his death, June 11, 1979, the *Western Livestock Journal* ran an obituary. "John Wayne," it began, "Hollywood box-office star and cattleman, is dead of cancer. He was 72."

This was the only reference to his "other" vocation. The rest of the obituary tells about his partnerships in the Red River Land and Cattle Company, and the 26 Bar Ranch. He is mentioned as one of the top breeders of registered Herefords in North America.

A few months before his death, bumper stickers blossomed out around the country, possibly a recognition of the Duke's battle with cancer. They said simply "God Bless John Wayne." A local merchant bought a supply of these and put them aside in an inconspicuous place. Possibly he was even a little embarrassed. After Wayne's death, he told me, people started to drift in and quietly buy them. Soon he was completely sold out.

Now the odd part. As far as I know, none of these bumper stickers have turned up on bumpers. I haven't seen even one.

I think people didn't want them for bumpers at all. They took them home to put carefully away somewhere. Then they can show them to their children and grandchildren some day, and tell them about it. About a time when America had some real heroes, and patriotism wasn't something to be ashamed of.

Ready for the Ring?

Of our five daughters, we've had five completely different personalities. I think they all thought they were expected to like horses, though that wasn't really essential. Some did, more than others. And some really did enjoy competing while some didn't. One of the girls loved working with the foals, and could clip and trim manes and tails to perfection. She just had no interest in getting into the show ring herself, though she loved to watch. And she was great at helping the others get ready.

A handy sort of a kid to have around.

And we had one years ago who came out of the ring crying one time when she took second in a big horsemanship class. I was embarrassed. I was sure everybody would think she was crying because she didn't win first. Actually, she was crying with happiness over placing that near the top. I was a little disgusted with her. I had seen the judge place her in *first*, and then change his mind because she was squirming around being "happy" at being in the top flight, instead of tending to business.

When we had three or four girls getting ready for the same horse show, it was a real hassle sometimes. Everyone had to be pretty much responsible for her own horse, clothes, and equipment. Some were good at this, some not so good.

One of our girls was a great talker. She'd carry on a conversation whether she knew anything about the subject or not. I used to think she'd be great in politics. This kid talked a fine horse race, but was just a little too lazy to really put forth the effort and work for it. Of course, the results were inevitable.

When she was about 12, she added another unpleasant personality trait. All girls sort of go crazy for a year or two at that age, I've noticed. In this case, our girl got careless and sloppy about her appearance. That was in the unbelievably Sloppy Sixties, anyway, but this kid really worked at it. And sloppy doesn't go in the horse show ring.

That spring she wasn't working her horse very much, and I finally called her attention to it. (Sure, sure, Dad, I'll have her ready.)

The date for the first show of the season approached. I checked with the girls as to whether we needed any new tack, and we got a few new items. This particular girl didn't need a thing. I knew her horse wasn't really ready for competition, but I thought I'd just let her learn the hard way, by making a fool of herself.

About ten minutes before her first class, the girl frantically sought me out. It was a Western Pleasure class, and chaps and a lariat were required. No, she hadn't forgotten her chaps. She'd just not tried them on, and her legs had grown so fat over the winter that she couldn't zip them. Fathers have to do a magic sometimes. I punched a few holes and tied her chaps on with bale twine. The day was saved.

When the contestants came into the ring, I was in for another shock. All the other contestants were dressed perfectly in fitted western outfits with shiny boots and new hats. Our girl was still wearing the old car coat she used to chore in, complete with bits of hay, dirt, and manure. Her hat was one that had blown into the pond a year before. The "lariat" on her saddle was an old piece of dirty cotton rope that we've used for years as a rump rope to teach foals to lead. All in all, the kid looked like she just spent the winter in a sheep camp somewhere. I hoped nobody would recognize the horse.

Naturally, the judge didn't even look at her. She came out of the ring at the end of the class. Now, I thought, she'll have learned a thing or two on a couple of subjects. But not so.

"Hi, Dad," she said cheerfully. "Ol' horse just wasn't working very well today!"

"Dark-Skinned People"

Among the joys of writing a regular column are some of the letters that are forwarded to me. Once in a while somebody really lands all over me like a duck on a June bug because I've stepped on a particular cherished belief. Maybe they think I've belittled their favorite breed of horse or given some sort of misinformation about it. Well, I probably did. There's a lot I don't know about horses. Sometimes I feel like the longer I'm around them, the less I know. Usually it works out okay. I always try to contact people who are really perturbed at me, and we find we're not too far apart. And sometimes I get another good subject for a column out of it.

But once in a while, I'll get a letter that is so heartwarming

Horse People

that it brings a tear to my eyes and really makes the whole thing worth while. After I wrote the article about Tom Bass, the world-famous negro horseman from Missouri, I received several comments about it. The most heartwarming was a letter from a girl in the Detroit area, who had seen the story in *Horse Of Course!* magazine.

"I'm nineteen," she wrote, "part negro and part Cherokee Indian. I've always been crazy about horses."

She went on to tell me that she had always avoided horses and horsemen, because at a very early age she was told, "horse people don't like dark-skinned people, so you just as well forget about it."

Now I thought that was pretty poor advice for anybody to give a youngster. This girl had, ever since, avoided an interest that would have afforded her many hours of pleasure. Of course, she still had the interest or she wouldn't be buying the magazine. She thought she might take another look at the horse thing.

I answered her letter. I told her I thought her information was incorrect. I've always considered horse people to be among the least likely to judge anyone unfairly on his background. In my experience, horsemen are more likely to judge by what sort of a person you are, and by your effort and ability, than anything else. I told her about some "dark-skinned" trainers, horse show judges, and rodeo contestants I've encountered, all well respected in their field. The fastest time at steer wrestling I ever saw (under 3 seconds) was by a big black cowboy at a bush league rodeo in Oklahoma. The crowd loved him. And the finest rodeo school in the world is operated by Jim Shoulders, an American Indian.

I told her to go ahead and take a crack at it, and to write me again when she wins her first ribbon at a horse show.

The girl didn't wait that long. She wrote to tell me that she'd found a horse she was sure would be the one she wanted, and was saving money to buy it. She'd apparently found people who were helping her with her interest. I'm sure a young person with this much enthusiasm will find people.

"This has changed my entire outlook on life," she writes.

"You are truly a beautiful person." (Aw, now, come on, that's carrying it a bit far — anyway, she hasn't *seen* me, you know.)

While writing this, another thought occurs to me. One of the other letters I received about the Tom Bass story was an interesting one from an old man who had been a friend of Mr. Bass. He had good memories of some of the specific horses he had seen Tom Bass work with in the ring. He wrote me twice — the second time to correct an error in the name of a mare he had mentioned.

But it suddenly occurred to me today — I don't know whether this gentleman was a *black* friend of Tom Bass or a white one. He didn't say, and I guess it just wasn't important.

The Small-Animal Man

I was doctoring a wire cut on one of our mares recently and remembered a similar accident many years ago.

One of our older daughters had a horse, a nice filly. The animal got a front foot in the fence and suffered a cut behind the fetlock, where they usually do. It bled a bit and looked awful, and I dried little-girl tears like a good daddy. We bandaged the foot, I gave the filly shots of tetanus toxoid and penicillin, and we fed her and put her in the stall.

That evening I got to thinking about the whole thing. I knew very little about doctoring horses. I'd worked with horses and mules a lot, but a lot of my experience was in the army where we had veterinarians available to take over any serious problems. I'd seldom been around horses with injuries, and I began to realize that I really didn't know much about what I was doing. I worried increasingly about it. What if there was something I should have done and hadn't? Or what if I did something I shouldn't have and something happened to the animal?

I finally decided I needed to consult with somebody who

knew. It would never do to get a bad result on a small daughter's horse.

Since this was long before we really got into the horse business, we didn't know any veterinarians. I didn't know who to call, but finally remembered an acquaintance who practiced veterinary medicine. His practice was limited to small animals, dogs and cats and such, but I figured he could help me. At least, I thought, he can advise me whether to call a local veterinarian or not.

I phoned him, apologized for bothering him with something really out of his line, and then got down to the question at hand. I described the injury, my attempts at a bandage, and told him what shots I'd given — tetanus toxoid and a shot of penicillin.

"My God!" he exploded, "You gave that horse a shot of *penicillin?*"

Oh, dear, I thought. I knew I'd done the wrong thing. Probably killed the filly. There must be something about horses that prevents the use of penicillin for them. I should have known, or at least I should have asked. How could I explain to a small girl that I had done wrong for her horse?

And what could it be? I'd never heard *not* to give penicillin to a horse. Apparently there was something about difference in species. But what could it be? I finally stammered an answer.

"Well, yes, I gave her . . . ."

"Don't ever give a shot of penicillin to a horse!" he practically shouted at me.

I was still puzzled. Surely I'd have heard something if this was an absolute no-no. I had to know.

"Why not?" I summoned courage to ask.

"They'll kick you!"

Well, I figured as he hung up and the dial tone came back on the line, now I know why his practice is limited to small animals!

The Natural-Born Rider

Horsin' Around Again

I didn't have any idea whether our grandson would have any interest in horses or not. If he didn't, that was okay. It's always been the same with our kids. Some did, some didn't, and it was okay with me either way.

Of course, he did seem to take a lot of interest in the spring-loaded play horse he got for his first Christmas. But most kids do like a play horse. Nathan wasn't quite a year old, but could soon bounce on it pretty well. Before long he graduated to a bigger horse his folks borrowed from friends.

He has two gaits on that one. Sometimes he bounces, just up and down, in what looks like a trot, but sometimes he rocks forward and back. The springs squeak and strain, and he throws his balance back and forward as the spring-horse leaps into a canter.

Meanwhile, when Nathan comes to see Grandpa and Grandma he sees real horses. He stands at the glass patio doors in the kitchen and can watch several horses come up to the fence about fifty feet away. That's where they're fed, so that's where they hang around when there's nothing better to do.

Of course he also likes to watch kittens, chickens, cows, and old Spot, so it keeps him pretty busy. He very quickly got the idea that a horse enjoys petting, too. He'll very gently pat a horse on the nose when it comes up to sniff him.

Then there was the parade. Nathan was about sixteen months old at the time of the Flint Hills Rodeo. By virtue of a number of other responsibilities, I wound up 1) late for the parade, and 2) baby-sitting Nathan. We did manage to watch most of the units in the parade march past at the end.

Nathan was all eyes. Here were hundreds of horses, all with people riding on them, and all happy and having fun. He was impressed. He was even more impressed when his Aunt Connie rode over to speak to us and sat there while he petted her horse's nose. He did a lot of jabbering about all this, and a lot of pointing. Nathan doesn't talk much, but it was plain he was telling me all about how much he liked the parade.

And then what was probably the high point of Nathan's day. A youngster who is a friend of ours had tied his pony to their trailer and we were all standing around visiting. I was holding Nathan, and reached over to put him in the pony's saddle for a moment. I didn't know what he'd do, but he was ready. He reached over, grabbed the other kid's cowboy hat, jammed it on his own head, and was ready to ride.

He shows in other ways that he appreciates horses, too. Connie set him on her horse the other day and led him a few steps. Nathan seemed to enjoy it, but didn't quite understand why she wouldn't let him have the reins! When the ride was over, he patted the saddle affectionately, and then leaned over to kiss the saddle horn. I'm sure he thinks the saddle is part of the horse, and was just thanking it for the ride.

Well, some people are born horsemen. Others work all their lives at it and are still only fair. I don't know how Nathan's going to do at this but I do know that he's sure trying hard, and that *he's* convinced he's a horseman.

Horsin' Around Again

The Centenarian

Well, the first guy to tell a story never has a chance. No sooner had I written the article about Alf Landon recently than I had another story. Governor Landon, at the age of 89, I had pointed out, rides his horse almost daily.

One of the first people who read that story reacted immediately. She, too, had long been an admirer of Alf Landon's, she told me. The former governor's horsemanship at 89 was especially interesting to her, since her own great-grandfather had been a horseman also. In fact, he had celebrated his 100th birthday by taking a ride. She had a photo and an old newspaper article to prove it and promised to show me both.

The clipping is from a newspaper in Troy, Kansas, dated March 26, 1924. It is entitled "Death of a Centenarian", and concerns the story of John Morehead, better known to residents of the community as Grandpa Morehead.

The story actually begins a couple of generations earlier, in the 1790's. John Morehead's grandfather saw a vision of a future in the "northwest", and moved his family from Maryland to Ohio by horseback. They had only one horse, so the young husband walked and led the horse. All their worldly goods were in a pack on the horse's back and atop this sat the wife, holding the baby. She had sewn a sort of pannier out of tow sacks, and this was thrown across the horse, under the pack. In each side of the sack was placed a small child, to balance the load. (That must have been some horse.)

One of the children in the tow sack was Calvin Morehead, father of our subject, John Morehead. John was born in Ohio on January 21, 1824. James Monroe was President of the United States, to be succeeded by John Quincy Adams that same year. Kansas, Mr. Morehead's future home, was a vague area on the map designated only as "Great American Desert." Napoleon had died only three years before, and Abraham Lincoln was nine years old.

John Morehead grew to manhood and married, moving

Horse People

restlessly to Indiana, Illinois, and finally deciding that his future lay in the west. In 1857 the Moreheads, with two small children, arrived at the frontier town of St. Joseph, Missouri, in a covered wagon. They crossed the Missouri River by ferry boat (there was no bridge) and settled in the Kansas Territory near where the town of Troy now stands.

He was a member of the Kansas Home Guard during the War Between the States. When Confederate General Price invaded the area and was repulsed at the Battle of Westport, Mr. Morehead's was one of the Home Guard units rushing to assist. They arrived an hour after the battle, however.

Although most of his life was spent in farming, John Morehead operated a freight service from Troy to St. Joseph for a number of years. He hauled the material to build the first Doniphan County Court House.

Retiring in 1893, the couple moved to town in 1901. Mrs. Morehead died in 1903, but Grandpa Morehead remained a well-known local figure for nearly another quarter of a century. It is difficult to visualize all the changes that took place during the lifetime of this man. At the time of his death, he had lived for over two-thirds of the entire history of the United States. His son's home, in which he spent his last days, was lighted by electricity and warmed by central heating. Quite a bit of progress for one lifetime, but remember, this man was born just after the time of Napoleon!

As mentioned above, Grandpa Morehead rode his horse to celebrate his 100th birthday. He had remained in good physical condition, as well as alert and with his mind clear. The photograph shows him to be straight and tall in the saddle. He sits a horse well, even at a hundred years of age. He appears to have had a pretty good horse, too.

A few months after the picture was taken, Grandpa Morehead died quietly at home. Here was a grand old pioneer, of whom descendents can be justly proud.

Red Cloud

To me, some of the most interesting features in the Emporia *Gazette* are the 20-years-ago, 40-years-ago, 60-years-ago columns. It's fun to read about what was considered important local news at that time, especially in the older items.

Some of the landmarks of sixty years ago have changed some in their importance to the community. Since this was in the days prior to the Anderson Fairgrounds, most of the summer activities seemed to be centered around Soden's Grove. I understand that there was a full-sized race track there at one time, with a grandstand, and harness racing at frequent intervals.

However, all this nostalgia is eclipsed by the "This Was the News" feature given me recently, clipped from the Leavenworth (Kansas) *Times*. Having been in continuous operation since 1857, the *Times* has 120 years of back files. Their column starts with "Ten Years Ago" and works back to "One Hundred Years Ago."

In some respects, things haven't changed much in a hundred years.

"The baseball fever is breaking out again," says the *Times* of March 18, 1877, "as winter seems to have virtually departed."

Another item deals with a more serious matter.

"Missouri Valley detectives followed some horse thieves into Wyandotte County yesterday. A man told where the hideout was. Several people were arrested near the Big Stranger Creek."

The gravity of this item is more apparent if we remember that a hundred years ago, horse theft in Kansas was punishable by hanging. And if any of the gang escaped, how would you like to have been the man who "told where the hideout was"?

An editorial comment from the century-old paper asks: "Why do our police continue to allow midnight prowling and shooting to be carried on in the heart of our city? Night before last there was a crowd of bums making the night hideous with their yelling on Main Street just north of the Planters House."

Horse People

I imagine the city police of some of the frontier towns really had their jobs cut out for them.

By far the most eloquent item for me, however, was this one:

"Red Cloud, the noted Indian warrior, will be in the city for a few days and proposes to sell three pens, three lead pencils, 10 sheets of commercial note paper, 10 envelopes, and a nickle plated penholder, all for 25 cents. We have tried them and liked them."

Now there's a real grabber for you. Red Cloud, "the noted Indian warrior. . . ." That was certainly an understatement.

Red Cloud was a war chief of the Oglala Sioux and one of their greatest leaders and patriots. His deeds of valor took a long time to recite in the ceremonials because of their great number. It is said that he once returned from a battle with the Crows with an arrow driven completely through his body, projecting front and back.

In 1865, the Sioux were asked to give up land between Fort Laramie and the gold fields in Montana. Red Cloud refused, and the army attempted to force the issue. Captain William J. Fetterman, who is quoted as having said, "Give me 80 men and I'll ride through the whole Sioux nation," tried to bring the Sioux into submission. A dazzling piece of military tactics by a group of Cheyenne, Arapaho, and Sioux under Red Cloud decoyed Captain Fetterman and his entire command into ambush and defeat.

For three years the standoff continued. Red Cloud could not be pushed aside, and the trail could not be used. In 1868, the U.S. Government surrendered, and the Black Hills and Powder River country were reserved for Red Cloud's people. The chief signed the treaty, and, true to his word, never made war on the whites again.

"You must begin anew and put away the wisdom of your fathers," he counseled his people.

And in 1877, Red Cloud sold pencils on the street in Leavenworth, Kansas.

Horsin' Around Again

The Expensive Cure

I can always pick up a story or two by spending a little time around horse people. Not long ago, our saddle club was running the gates, ticket sales, and concessions stand at the quarter horse races out at the fairgrounds. In the course of the day I got to talking with a couple of fellows who had grown up around horses. One was telling about his dad's methods for doctoring sick horses.

A drench with ginger and maybe a shot of whiskey was the cure for colic. The mixture was poured into a pop bottle. The horse's head was lifted and held with a twitch so that the liquid could be poured into a corner of the animal's mouth. (A "twitch", for the uninitiated, is a thong or cord around the upper lip, twisted tightly enough with a stick to distract the horse from moving around.)

Various sorts of liquid medicine were given with a bottle in this way. Some seem pretty unlikely. Turpentine, for instance, was a cure for worms. Tobacco was used for the same purpose, either just chewing tobacco "as is", or soaked in water, alcohol, whiskey, kerosene, or turpentine and given as a drench. Every horseman had his favorite recipe, I suppose.

Another story involved the treatment of "fistula." This was a problem with work horses wearing a collar. A sore would develop from the rubbing of the collar. Because of the way a horse's muscles and connective tissue are constructed around the shoulder, the wound would extend. With gravity preventing drainage, an infected tract would develop deep into the shoulder. Sometimes the horse would become permanently useless.

One of my friends at the races was describing how his father opened the upper end of the fistula with his knife, placed two dimes in the wound, and a stitch or two to hold them in. My friend was a pretty small boy at the time, and he was mostly impressed with the extravagance of using that much money for such a purpose. It's true that would have been enough for a pretty fair meal for most families then. Incidentally, he couldn't remember whether the treatment worked or not. He was too concerned over the loss of the coins.

Another man in the conversation observed that he had seen fistula treated similarly with a stick. I've heard of that. A pencil-sized twig of peeled, slippery elm was inserted from the top end. Theoretically, as the wound healed from the bottom, it would push the stick out a little at a time.

Slippery elm was thought to possess remarkable medicinal properties. I can remember my grandfather describing treatment of human eye injuries with a poultice of slippery elm bark, chewed into a mush by the patient. He credited this with saving one of his eyes after an accident.

An interesting finale to the conversation at the race track concerned the same man who used the dimes to treat fistula. He had raised and trained work horses for many years. In those days, the entire economy of the nation revolved around the use of the draft horse to produce, harvest, and transport all the gross national product. There was always a good market for the teams he raised.

Then came a day when he returned from working in the field, hung up the harness, and turned out the team, as usual. Next day, without a word of explanation to anybody, he sold out everything and went back to school to become a preacher.

Well, I can understand that. There are times when working with horses can be enough to drive a person to drink. Or into the ministry.

Nostalgia Ain't What It Was

A Winter Adventure

We recently spent a short vacation visiting our daughter April and her husband. This was the first time we had visited in their present location, and it was an unusual experience, to say the least.

Mike is working for a large ranching operation in northwest Colorado, and April was fortunate enough to find a teaching job in the same area. Her school is the Brown's Park School, eight grades in one room, and I think she has about nine students. What, you didn't know there were still schools like that? Neither did I! April tells us there are three or four, at least.

Her letter with directions on how to find their home is a masterpiece. I saved it for future reference. We got off the Interstate Highway, I-70, at Rifle, Colorado. (That sound remote? Just wait!) Following directions, we headed north toward Meeker, about 50 miles. I began to feel some stirrings of historical interest. Meeker, Colorado, is named for N. C. Meeker, an Indian agent who was killed by the Utes in 1879. The bone of contention was that the agent kept insisting that they break their horses to harness and teach them to plow. That wasn't the worst. The area he chose to plow for potatoes happened to be the race track. Agent Meeker was opposed to horse racing as a sinful occupation.

To enforce his edict, Meeker announced that all rations would be withheld until the Indians complied. This unwise decision resulted in a Ute uprising which left Meeker and dozens of others dead, both red and white. You can't starve people into cooperation.

The remote vastness of the country we were traveling through reminded us that Meeker's debacle wasn't really all that long ago. After some zigging and zagging near Meeker, we found the sign we were looking for:

> Strawberry
> Wilson Creek
> Price Creek

"Turn right and go 15 miles," our instructions said, "to the gravel road, 13 miles on gravel, and 12 miles on pavement." Such details would have been unnecessary. There wasn't a place we could have turned off that road after the "Strawberry, etc." sign.

"Turn left 1¼ miles to Maybell. A half mile out of Maybell is the turnoff to Sunbeam on Highway 318."

Well, we found that turn, and there was a sign which read:

> Caution
> No services
> next 100 miles

Hell's bells, I told Edna, there haven't been any for the *last* hundred miles!

"Stay on 318 for about 40 miles," the letter continued, "and you'll see a sign:

> "Brown's Park 5 miles

"From that sign it is 10 miles to our house."

Now, that last 50 miles sounds simple enough, right? It wasn't hard. Again, there wasn't any sort of wrong turn we *could* have taken in the entire distance. Just the ribbon of 318 slicing through the night. There were a few complicating factors. Three times I had to slam on the brakes to avoid hitting deer, once a herd of nearly a dozen animals.

Then, this is also open range country. The state highway has metal cattle guards across it at intervals, and there may be stock on the highway at any point. A very cautious speed, especially at night, was a must.

Once we were startled by a bunch of horses. They were on both sides of the road, and seemed completely unconcerned as we drove past. We heard later that there are about 700 horses which are wintered in that area and leased in the summer to various dude ranches.

Nostalgia Ain't What It Was

Anyway, we didn't hit any deer, or horses, or any other livestock. We found the kids' place, and enjoyed a late supper of rich venison stew.

I was looking forward to the next day. Here was country I've read about all my life. The country of the old Outlaw Trail, the Hole in the Wall Gang, Butch Cassidy, and the Sundance Kid. I was eager as a kid at Christmas.

 Butch Cassidy's Yard

Brown's Park (formerly Brown's Hole) isn't a town, or a settlement, but a place. Lying roughly east-west, the Park is about 50 or 60 miles long and two to six wide, more or less. Geologically, it is unique for the area. Elevation, for instance, is much lower than the surrounding territory, lower even than Denver. This produces a much milder climate in winter than most of the rest of northwest Colorado. Almost a "banana belt," one resident told me. (That's exaggerating a little.)

The Green, a magnificent mountain river, rushes out of Utah and through most of the length of Brown's Park. It is joined en route by Vermillion Creek and several smaller springfed creeks. The Green River leaves the Park through a frightening gash in the mountain called the Gates of Lodore. Here the fast, treacherous current narrows and moves even faster, crashing between sheer granite walls to produce a jetlike effect, exactly as the nozzle on a fire hose does.

The wild beauty of this place, the mild climate, and the constant water supply of the Green have apparently attracted people for many centuries. There are prehistoric pictographs carved into the cliffs, if one knows where to look. A granite cube the size of a small house stands as a monolith in one area near the Gates of Lodore. A bronze tablet fastened to the rock states that here Jim Bridger and various other mountain men and

Indians used to hold winter rendezvous. Directly beneath the bronze plate is a series of the prehistoric pictographs. They are human figures of varying sizes, and undoubtedly the message is similar to that in bronze, telling of prehistoric mountain men.

In later years, settlers came to winter livestock in the shelter of the valley. Not many. It's still a cruel, tough, inaccessible country. This inaccessibility made it a haven for outlaws for many years, a station on the "Outlaw Trail", the mythical "road" for men on the run. The Outlaw Trail was very real, however, and stopovers like Rock Springs, Wyoming, and Brown's Hole were used by dozens of famous desperadoes.

"Brown's Hole" became "Brown's Park" through the efforts of Elizabeth Bassett, an early settler who felt that the valley was too beautiful to be called a hole. She insisted that in her presence, people must call it a "park." Mrs. Bassett became such a respected and admired citizen that she was actually able to enforce this idea, and it has been Brown's Park ever since. Incidentally, Elizabeth Bassett died at 37, victim of what may have been appendicitis. There was no doctor in the Park, but this would have been before the time of surgery for appendicitis, anyway.

Brown's Park had its range wars, too, over the years. Ann Bassett, a daughter of Elizabeth, was actually tried for cattle rustling and acquitted in 1913. This girl, known as "Queen Ann" to the local people, was a striking personality. She was raised, almost literally, in the bunkhouse, but attended the finest of Boston finishing schools. Her self-appointed mission in life was the harassment of the Two Bars Ranch, which to her represented all that was evil of the big cattle barons. Local legend has it that on one occasion, she and her cowboys were driving 250 head of stolen Two Bars cattle when they found themselves cornered by a posse.

Expert horsemen that they were, they drove the entire herd over a bluff into the river just above the yawning mouth of the Gates of Lodore. This effectively destroyed all evidence, and the posse returned empty-handed.

The job of our son-in-law is to look after several hundred cattle belonging to Watson Ranches, Inc. He must know about how many cows are in which area and move them if they stray. This could involve a distance of quite a few miles.

I rode out in the pickup with him one morning to check on cattle. We parked on a high mesa and Mike scanned the valley with his binoculars.

"Oh, they're back in Butch's yard again," he said. "We'll have to go move them back west a ways tomorrow."

Butch? Butch Cassidy, of course. There's a tumbling-down log cabin on the south bank of the Green that is said to have belonged to the famous outlaw.

Real Cowboyin'

Early next morning, after feeding the bulls and the replacement heifers, Connie and I joined Mike to go herd the cows out of "Butch Cassidy's yard." The cabin is only a mile and a half from their house, but it's across the Green River, and that makes it a little complicated. The Green is such a rugged, treacherous stream that there's only one bridge across it in the entire state of Colorado. That was several miles west of us, almost to the Utah line. We drove out to the bridge.

What a bridge! Over 300 feet long, the suspension bridge hangs on a slim pair of cables, over a hundred feet above the gorge. It is possible to cautiously drive a pickup truck across by folding the side mirrors down, it's that narrow. The sign on the bridge says:

> Caution: Weight limit
> 30 cattle
> 200 sheep
> 2½ tons

We cautiously drove across and the bridge floor undulated in waves ahead of us. I thought for a moment of the story of what had happened to the original bridge before this one was built. It had been whipped to pieces when it got to swinging wildly in a windstorm.

The pickup headed back east on what is optimistically referred to as a road, strewn with pumpkin-sized boulders. We proceeded in 4-wheel for several miles. "The horses ought to be about here," Mike observed. He had turned two horses out on the other side of the river so he wouldn't have to haul them over each time he needed them. Since there were no fences, the horses could run about anywhere on the Western Slope, but they were right where Mike expected. We caught and saddled them with the aid of a bucket of oats.

Mike's horse was called Big John, which seemed as good a name as any for a big rawboned bay. The other, to be used by Connie, was Carl Williams. The practice of naming a horse after its previous owner is still very common in the west. In this case, the horse had been acquired from Carl Williams, whoever he might be. Anyway, the name belongs to the horse now.

I had elected to drive the pickup. I didn't think I was in shape for the kind of cowboying this might take. To start the gather, we moved on down to "Butch's" place and paused to look around.

The cabin had been a pretty good-sized structure, probably had three rooms. It was certainly an eerie feeling to stand in the doorway and look across the bend of the Green at the cottonwoods in the meadow. It must have looked nearly identical when Butch himself stood there. Now, I don't know for a fact that this is Butch Cassidy's cabin, you understand. Local tradition says it is.

I stood there, leaning against the doorway and reflecting on the secure inaccessibility of the place. Something half-buried in the sand caught my eye. An old brass cartridge case, corroded to a dusty blue-green color. It is 45-70 caliber, which could certainly correspond to usage during Cassidy's day. Was it fired by one of the "Wild Bunch" or perhaps Butch himself? Was it fired for practice, for meat, or was there a human target? (Butch Cassidy, incidentally, never killed anyone in his life.)

Mike and Connie rounded up the few cows in the area and

started them back west along the river. I followed in the 4-wheel-drive pickup, using low gears most of the way. By the time Mike had rousted cows out of various gullies and brush along the river, the gather had grown to a hundred head or more. We pushed them several miles toward the bridge, and then up into the foothills where the grass was better.

"I s'pose," observed Mike, "they'll be back in a day or two, and I'll have to chase 'em again."

We unsaddled Carl and Big John, and they ambled off to look for grass.

In that part of the country, cowboyin' hasn't really changed a lot, except that you can do part of it from a pickup truck.

New Year's Party

One of the most unusual parties I ever attended was in Brown's Park. As New Year's Eve approached, we had heard there was to be a community party, so April phoned a neighbor to find out about it.

Yes, they said, be sure to come. Bring snack food and anything you want to drink. Breakfast will be served at $2 each. The party was at Lodore Hall, an old school building now used as a community center, standing alone on Vermillion Creek and with no sign of civilization in sight.

We got there about 9:30, and people were just beginning to arrive in vehicles of all sorts. A roaring fire of cottonwood logs was heating the old iron stove and the hall was warming rapidly.

A sign at the door said: "No beer, liquor, or other alcoholic beverages permitted inside."

Directly under the sign stood a smiling fellow who welcomed us warmly.

"Hi! C'mon in! Just put your bottles on that table, and your food on that one over there. Help yourself to anybody's!"

The food table was already groaning with cheeses, crackers, dips, sausages, and hors d'oeuvres. Great food, too. Everything from caviar to homemade summer sausage.

By the time people stopped arriving, there were maybe fifty there. Goodlooking, well-dressed people. They ranged in age from about six months to past seventy. Naturally, I thought. Where could anyone find a baby-sitter out here? You just had to take the kids along. This group apparently included nearly every human being between Sunbeam, Colorado and Vernal, Utah. I was told they were about half Mormons and half Catholics, but it didn't seem to matter. Primarily, they were people, here to visit, dance, and see the New Year in.

The music was supplied by a loosely-organized band, headed by the Park Ranger from over at the Gates of Lodore. Other members included a young rancher from down the river, a septuagenarian from over in Utah, and a guy from Taylor Flats. (I met all these people in the course of the evening, but never did get a name for the last mentioned. Everyone I asked just said, "Oh, him? That's the guy from Taylor Flats.")

After some dancing, eating, and visiting, it became apparent that the band had a slight problem. They had a washtub string bass, but didn't seem to have anyone to play it. A couple of people tried it for a number or two, but the string kept slipping, and finally it was just left standing there. Being an old tub-bass virtuoso, I offered my services, and was welcomed aboard. It was really a pretty well-built instrument, and I got it adjusted properly before long. I found I could even do a run on it sometimes, much to the amusement of my family. Especially my son-in-law, who had never seen me play one before.

Everybody danced with everybody. Teenage girls danced with ranchers in their seventies. Eighth-grade boys solemnly asked middle-aged ladies to dance, and were seriously accepted. One couple danced, holding a six-month-old baby in their arms. The little head looked over mom's shoulder and bobbed around with a delighted grin on his face, swaying in time to the music.

As youngsters began to tire, they were put to bed in a row

along one side of the hall, with blankets and coats thrown over them. There they slept through the rest of the party.

Time passes quickly when you're having fun. Midnight came and went, and breakfast was announced at 2:00 A.M. We all lined up for ham, eggs, and a stack of flapjacks prepared by the women's club. ("Just put your money in that black hat over there on the table.")

Then the band tuned up and people started dancing again!

"Look," I said, "we've got to go! We have to start home tomorrow."

We rounded up the family and departed. When we left, people were still happily dancing to the guitars of the Park Ranger and the guy from Taylor Flats.

Run, Spot, Run!

I've often said that everybody has a horse story to tell, and I picked up this one only recently from a guy whom I've known for years.

Back in the thirties, people tried some pretty strange horse-breeding projects, and the result of such a cross was a little mare on the farm of my friend's neighbor. Her mother was a pinto shetland pony, and her sire was a Thoroughbred stallion. The mare was a bit on the small side, from her pony mother, but fast as lightning, from her race-horse father. Her owner used her in impromptu races and did quite well at it. At that time there were thousands of bush-league races in the country. Many were informal, "my horse can beat your horse" type contests, with stock saddles, and the owner or some local kid acting as jockey.

The little pinto mare looked so unassuming that she was really good at this type of racing. No one who looked at the mare was likely to take her racing ability seriously because she didn't *look* like a race horse, and her owner could get pretty good odds out of the big boys with the expensive horses.

As the years passed, Spot (it was mandatory to call any paint horse "Spot") decided she really liked this racing thing. She didn't want to do anything else *but* race! The mare would try to run away every time someone climbed on her back. By the time she was 10 or 12 years old, her speed was waning, and younger horses began to beat her occasionally. Spot's owner retired her to pasture.

At this point my friend enters the story. He was a kid about ten, and used to fish in the creek that ran through Spot's pasture. The horse was lonesome for company, and the two struck up a sort of friendship. Eventually, the boy got up enough nerve to ask the owner if he'd sell Spot. No, he was told, but he could have her, with the understanding that she was no kid horse and might run away with the rider.

Spot, by this time, had other ideas. She loved kids, and turned out to be a real kid horse. They could ride her double, triple, bareback, or any other way, and unless the situation looked like a race, she'd never try to run with the youngsters.

A few years later, an unusual attraction arrived at the County Fair. A man dressed in a track suit offered to bet $25 that he could outrun anyone's race horse for 25 yards! Now this requires a bit of explanation. At that short a distance, almost any good sprinter can outrun a horse. It takes the horse several strides to hit his speed, and by that time the runner has crossed the wire. Most people don't realize this fact, and the betting was heavy, with the carnival man consistently beating all comers.

My friend and his brothers watched most of an afternoon. Finally they approached their father.

"Dad," they confided, "we think old Spot can beat this guy!"

After watching a few more races, the father agreed, and sent them home for Spot, while he placed his hard-earned $25 bet. The little mare immediately recognized this as a race and curiously examined her opponent — the man in the track suit!

Now there are those horsemen who will loudly defend the principle that a small horse has an advantage in the first jump or two out of the starting gate. Mechanically, it takes a shorter time to bunch and extend a shorter leg, and this is why many small horses are cat-quick on their feet.

At the first sign of motion on the part of her opponent, Spot leaped forward, using her old race-horse experience in good stead. She beat the runner in three or four long leaps, and the crowd went wild.

The match became an annual event in the county, with Spot winning each year. The carnival man was glad to have a horse who could win occasionally, to keep interest up, and the boys could certainly use the small but relatively sure annual income. And Spot? Well, she always enjoyed a good race.

Dining on Horseback

There's a trend right now for young couples to write their own wedding ceremony. In a way, I sort of like this. I think it may be much more meaningful a contract if they have given it some thought. The traditional old-fashioned ceremony somehow loses its punch through repetition. Our own resulted in the tying of a quite solid knot, I'll admit. Still, I can see how contemporary couples can enjoy writing their own. And we've been to some beautiful contemporary weddings recently.

Some get a little far out. I don't know where you'd draw the line. Outdoors is nice, but I'd stop maybe a little short of having the groomsmen barefoot and with flowers in their hair. Likewise, I view with mixed emotion the weddings under water in scuba equipment, and in balloons, or on basketball courts, etc. Yes, even on horseback. I heard of one like that recently. Incidentally, it would appear that the occupational hazards of the ministry are proliferating at an alarming pace.

As far as marriage is concerned, I think there's a major thing the young couple must realize. That marriage license is no guarantee of happiness. It's just a permit to *look* for it. More like a hunting license, actually. Success isn't guaranteed, but depends on patience, insight, and hard work.

But back to the horseback marriage ceremony. I guess practically anything can be done on horseback. We see horseback church services on rodeo weekends quite frequently in recent years. I've seen a little girl lying full length on the back of a grazing horse and reading a book.

The American Indians, I'm told, used an old mare as a babysitter. Baby was simply tied on the back of a dependable animal and turned out to graze. It's little wonder that they could ride before they could walk.

Recently, however, an event was called to my attention that is really the ultimate in horseback activity. Dinner on horseback. Not that eating on horseback is unusual, you understand. Almost everybody who ever spent much time in a saddle has done it. You cram sandwiches or cold biscuits or apples or candy bars in your pockets and saddle bags. This is a handy way to avoid missing lunch when you know you're going to miss lunch. Washed down with cold Flint Hills spring water and maybe a sprig of watercress out of the spring, it goes pretty good. But all that's not the point.

Recently Mrs. W. L. White, wife of the late Emporia *Gazette* publisher, sent me an interesting picture. She'd found it among Mr. White's things. It was taken in 1903 by a photographer named Byron. There is no other information as to the circumstances or who the people in the picture may be. It is simply a "Horseback Dinner at Sherry's Restaurant", the New York City emporium of *haute cuisine*.

And what a dinner! Full dress, no less, in what appears to be a ballroom. There are about twenty-five elderly gentlemen, each seated on his horse, facing center in a large circle. Each is wearing a tuxedo. No jodhpurs or boots, just the long trousers of a formal dress outfit. Some of the jackets even appear to be the long-tailed Prince Albert style.

From the build of the horses, this may have been a hunt club or something of the sort. Several saddle blankets are visible, all precisely alike, heavily embroidered or decorated.

Sherry's must have really gone all-out for the occasion. There is a thick layer of sawdust on the floor, and a lot of potted shrubbery. In the center of the circle is a potted palm that must be twelve feet tall.

Over the pommel of each saddle is a sort of table, like the thing a hospital patient has over the bed. I can't tell from the picture whether they're fastened to the horse or to the floor. Between each pair of horses is a flight of steps, to allow the waiters to serve the various courses. And waiters, standing attentively behind, are dressed in white riding pants, boots, and hunt jackets.

Well, okay, whatever's cool.

Jim Key, the Educated Horse

I recently ran across a horse story that would make a great movie, except that nobody would believe it. It's even a bit far-out for the Disney-type animal movies.

Few people now living remember that around the turn of the century one of the most popular animal acts in the world was a horse — Jim Key, the "Educated Horse."

The colt's mother was an Arabian mare, trained in the 1880's as a circus performer. His sire was Tennessee Volunteer, winner of the famed Hambletonian, brightest jewel in the harness racing circuit. A few photographs in existence show Jim Key to have a rather long build and a Thoroughbred-type head. Jim's owner was Dr. William Key, DVM, a black veterinarian.

"For nearly a year after Jim was foaled," he later recalled, "we had no hope for him. He near broke my heart, for he was the most spindly, shank-legged animal I ever did see."

The story might have ended right there if Jim had had any other owner. But Dr. Key was a believer in kindness, patience, and understanding in training horses (a rather unusual idea at

103

the time, I imagine). Instead of destroying the foal as a useless specimen, the doctor took it to the house. The colt was named after a neighbor of Key's whom he described as "a no-account bowlegged nigger named Jim."

"I took good care of him, and before long his legs began to straighten out," the story continued. "He just lived in the house and followed me around like a dog. He wanted to know what everything was, and I commenced to teach him simple things. One of the first things he learned, and I didn't teach him that, either, was to unfasten the gate and let himself out."

The colt learned rapidly, and the "hopeless-looking creature" developed an astounding repertoire of tricks. According to Dr. Key, no "whip, stick or angry words" were ever used on the horse. He learned eagerly and soon began to give public exhibitions.

There have been a number of "educated" horses in history. One of the most famous was Hans, the "Wonder Horse" of Germany. Hans could spell, count, and do simple arithmetic problems. For a while it was thought that the trainer was cueing the horse. Ultimately Hans was found to have the ability to perform even with only strangers present. It has been suggested that perhaps there is some telepathic message that the horse picks up. Someone has to know the answer in order to ask the question, and the horse may "read" his thoughts. Far be it from me to say it couldn't happen. No trickery was ever uncovered.

In the case of Jim Key, the horse is said to have given exhibitions in reading, writing, spelling, counting, figuring, money changing, telling time, and "a score of other traits." He was exhibited all over the United States for a number of years. At the St. Louis Exposition in 1904, Jim Key drew more paid admissions than any other show. He was valued at $100,000 — quite a fortune at that time. Many celebrities saw the horse perform. A special fan was John Philip Sousa, the famous bandmaster.

Jim Key lived to the age of 27, a ripe old age for a horse. He died in 1918, shortly after the death of his owner and friend, Dr. William Key. He was buried on the Key farm in Tennessee.

Nostalgia Ain't What It Was

Runaway!

One of the most spectacular sights in the days when most transportation was by horse power must have been a runaway. Horses, young horses especially, are sometimes flighty and nervous, and may "spook" unexpectedly at some unfamiliar object. A young horse in training is much more likely to do so.

The offending object might be anything — a scrap of blowing paper, an odd-shaped rock, a stick, or just light and shadow, or a wisp of grass stirred by a stray breeze. I understand that one of the major hazards to circus bareback performers in the days of the Big Top was the ever-present possibility of a tiny pinhole in the tent. Dust motes, dancing in a beam of sunlight through the hole, would confuse the galloping horses, and they would shy or attempt to hurdle the sunbeam.

A runaway team hitched to a wagon, however, could be a serious matter to everyone. For instance, a heavy draft team might weigh a couple of tons in horses alone, plus the weight of the freight wagon and its load. You can imagine the destruction this could produce on a busy city street.

Or consider, for example, a farm youngster driving a half-trained team pulling farm machinery. A runaway with a mowing machine was a terrifying experience. The sickle bar, with the whirring little knives spurring frightened horses on, stuck out several feet to the right of the machine, and would slice through anything in its path, including livestock, dogs, poultry, or people. A runaway with a plow or cultivator might not be quite as bad, since it would require so much more effort on the part of the horses, and they would tire faster. I do recall a friend telling me about his dad working him over with the lines. He had made the mistake of letting a half-wild team run away with the cultivator and had torn up a strip of young corn.

This was the major reason for harnessing an experienced old horse with a young one in training, to steady the youngster and show him the job.

Runaways on a buggy were something spectacular. Buggies

were fairly light and consequently fairly fragile, and a runaway team or single horse in harness could smash wheels, overturn the buggy, or tear up a lot of expensive harness. There was always a certain amount of danger to life and limb, both to drivers and to passengers, as well as to pedestrians and other vehicles. My wife's grandmother died in her forties as a result of injuries received in a runaway.

My mother-in-law tells reminiscently of driving the family buggy to town each week with a load of eggs and cream, and having the old horse repeatedly run away, across ditches and fields. She says sometimes there would be hardly any eggs broken. (Now if this were my story, I think I'd tell how the cream was always churned to butter when we got to town. But, it's Grandma's story.)

I'm sure that numerous young men used to instigate a runaway occasionally to demonstrate for the girls their ability to stop one. And it would be about as easy to fake a runaway with a good fast team. All you'd have to do would be to spook them up pretty good, holler "Runaway!", and attract a lot of public attention while you expertly brought the team under control. This would be akin to the present-day practice of "peeling rubber" for half a block after stopping at a stop light. It was probably done by similar young men, for similar reasons, and drew very much the same sort of reaction from the onlookers. Even at that, I guess it makes about as much sense as teenage cyclists "popping wheelies."

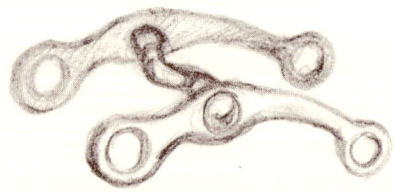

Nostalgia Ain't What It Was

Code of the Cowboy

I have a theory about the reason for the big nostalgia thing in recent years. Part of it is the backwash of the Bicentennial, of course, but it's more than that. It's a sort of longing for a return to a time when things were simpler. And slower, maybe. I saw the results of a poll a year or two ago which indicated that over half the people questioned were actually *enjoying* the 55 mile speed limit. Well, you certainly can see more at 55 than at 75.

And things used to be not only slower but simpler, too. We used to be able to feel that there were some things that were solid and lasting and simple. God, country, motherhood, and apple pie seemed pretty permanent, along with J. Edgar Hoover's FBI and the U.S. currency.

Now things have changed. How long has it been since the phrase "sound as a dollar" had any meaning? The FBI and the police are being bad-mouthed, along with the CIA, for not being nice to the *bad guys*! Of course, it's harder to tell the bad guys from the good guys now. The good guys don't all wear white hats. Of the other values listed, God's name can't be mentioned in school, and we're getting used to hearing our country criticized by our own leaders. Motherhood is even suspect, due to the population crisis. As for apple pie, it may be hazardous to your health because of a miniscule amount of some additive found to be cancer-producing (based on studies carried out on a group of three male wombats in Tasmania).

No wonder we find ourselves wishing for a return to a simpler set of values. We don't have many folk heroes left, but we do have a couple.

Several months ago ABC aired a TV special, "Stars' Tribute to John Wayne." One of the high points of the show was the reading, by Jimmy Stewart and Sammy Davis, Jr., of a poem, "Code of the Cow Country." It was erroneously attributed to an Odessa, Texas man, but ABC later rectified the mistake. The poem was written by S. Omar Barker, one of the grand old western writers of this century.

107

Horsin' Around Again

This little poem has an illustrious history, and you may have run across it before. It was first published in 1929 in *Western Story Magazine* and later reprinted in two of Mr. Barker's books. It has been selected for several western anthologies. This is the sort of thing that is so simple and to-the-point that the first time we see it, we say to ourselves, "Boy, I wish I'd said that!" Then we can continue to go back and enjoy it again. Here is the poem, enjoyed by America for nearly a half century.

Code of the Cow Country*
by S. Omar Barker

It don't take such a lot of laws
    To keep the rangeland straight,
Nor books to write 'em in, because
    There's only six or eight.
The first one is the welcome sign—
    True brand of Western hearts:
My camp is yours and yours is mine
    In all cow country parts.

Treat with respect all womankind
    Same as you would your sister.
Take care of neighbors' strays you find,
    And don't call cowboys "mister."
Shut pasture gates when passin' through,
    And takin all in all,
Be just as rough as pleases you,
    But never mean or small.

Talk straight, shoot straight and never break
    Your word to man or boss.
Plumb always kill a rattlesnake.
    Don't ride a sorebacked hoss.
It don't take laws nor pedigree
    To live the best you can.
These few are all it takes to be
    A cowboy — and a man!

*Copyright by the author, used here by special permission.

Nostalgia Ain't What It Was

The Mountain Wedding

As part of the current nostalgia for the simplicity of an earlier day, we are seeing a revival of a lot of old-time skills. People are learning to knit, weave, whittle, spin, churn, and a host of other frontier occupations. I've often thought that the current increasing interest in the horse is part of this nostalgia.

There are a number of groups around the country that combine several of these skills to create a replica of one of the most fascinating American frontier types: the "Mountain Man." The names of Jim Bridger, Kit Carson, Hugh Glass, and Jed Smith are enough to send a thrill up the spine of any red-blooded American boy. These men were known and respected by the Indians, were experts at their craft. They were trackers, explorers, trappers, superb horsemen, and excellent marksmen with their muzzle-loading rifles.

Interest in this variety of accomplishments has prompted the formation of such organizations as the Rocky Mountain Fur Company. This group holds a rendezvous and competitive shooting match periodically in the historic Brown's Park area where Bridger and the others of the original Rocky Mountain Fur Company met.

Understand, this isn't just a bunch of grown-ups playing Daniel Boone. It's pretty hard to get into the Rocky Mountain Fur Company. First, an applicant has to *build* his muzzle-loading rifle, either flintlock or cap and ball. These rifles are usually .50 to .58 caliber, with a fairly short, heavy barrel. They are the plains and mountain adaptation of the long "Kentucky" rifles, shortened for use on horseback. The caliber is larger, for the larger game of the west.

Our applicant must now use his rifle to kill a deer or elk and tan the skin, using Indian methods of course. From this buckskin he then makes his authentic mountain man costume. Some of these fringed and beaded outfits are truly beautiful. A real purist will refrain from the use of scissors and needles, sewing with sinew and a bone awl.

Horsin' Around Again

The applicant must construct a teepee and decorate it with natural dyes. A teepee, incidentally, is one of the most comfortable and versatile dwellings ever devised.

In mid-February, 1977, an event took place that was unique even for the Rocky Mountain Fur Company — a wedding. We were not privileged to attend, but our daughter April sent us the writeup from the Craig, Colorado *Press*.

The groom, Lee Robertson, is president of the Fur Company and works for the Utah Game and Fish Department. The mountain men had assembled on Saturday, February 12, and pitched a dozen or more teepees along the bank of the Green River. A large buckskin-clad man with black handlebar moustaches rode into camp, leading a packhorse. He was Rev. J. D. Waddle of Arvada, Colorado, known throughout the area as "The Circuit-Ridin' Preacher." Waddle is pastor of the Valley Bible Baptist Church, and has made his circuit-riding activities an important part of his ministry.

The circuit rider produced an accordion from the horse's pack and led his flock in a hymn, "Shall We Gather at the River." Following this, the traditional wedding ceremony took place, uniting Mr. Robertson in marriage to Alice Oliver of Salt Lake City. A number of the mountain men took the opportunity to renew their vows with their own wives.

A reception held in the middle of the teepee camp provided chile and hot cider. The group watched the bride and groom step into a canoe and paddle off down the Green on their honeymoon, amid whoops and rifle shots from the shore.

Actually, the couple returned that evening for the formal Indian Council fire, followed by a dance at Lodore Hall, mountain man style, of course. That must have been a great weekend.

Nostalgia Ain't What It Was

Pony Express

WANTED
Young, skinny, wiry fellows, not over eighteen.
Must be expert riders, willing to risk death daily.
Orphans preferred.
Wages $25 per week.
Apply Pony Express Stables
St. Joseph, Missouri.

★★★★

The above handbill, with a picture of a wildly-galloping horse and rider, appeared in hundreds of western towns in 1860. The Pony Express became a thrilling chapter in American history.

Conceived by a trio of partners, Messrs. Russell, Majors, and Waddell, the Express was an attempt to speed delivery of mail to the west coast. The route stretched from St. Joseph, Missouri, to Sacramento, California, a distance of nearly 2,000 miles. Delivery time for first class mail could be shortened considerably, the founders figured, by having carefully-selected men and horses waiting along the route. Each rider was to cover a lap of 75 to 100 miles, changing horses six to eight times enroute. The speedy change was accomplished by means of special equipment. An apron-like *mochila*, of special leather, was designed to fit over the saddle, with only the horn and cantle protruding. Four locked leather cases on the skirts of the *mochila* held the mail.

The average time for the entire run was about 10 days. The fastest run carried President Lincoln's inaugural address, and was completed in 7 days, 17 hours.

Horses were specially selected for the Express. There was a tendency to use hot-blooded Kentucky stock for the eastern portions of the route, and tough western mustangs for the more rugged mountains and deserts. These horses, several hundred in number, were to receive the best in feed and care, but the extremely hard work resulted in many casualties. Purchase of replacements was a common expense in the operation.

The all-important feature of the enterprise was the motto: *The mail must go through.* The schedule was the prime factor, and riders were urged to adhere to schedule despite any obstacles. These could include bad weather, treacherous trails and streams, wild animals, and outlaws, renegades, or hostile Indians. The "orphans preferred" stipulation in the handbill was a very serious and practical matter. The Express did not intend to be harassed by bereaved families of their employees.

All told, about 120 young men were hired as riders. Perhaps the most famous of these was William F. (Buffalo Bill) Cody. Many of the riders on the western half of the route were young Mormons from the Utah settlements.

Apparently the first riders actually wore a uniform of red shirt, blue pants, broad-brimmed hat, and boots. Most carried a pistol and wore spurs. Later riders wore more informal dress of their own choosing.

The Pony Express was a spectacular success in the sense that mail delivery was proved possible in ten days or less. A government contract for U.S. mail was awarded the Express, much to the discomfiture of the Butterfield Stage line which had held a previous contract for a mail stage route further south.

From a practical standpoint the project was doomed to oblivion anyway. Within a year and a half, the telegraph spanned the continent, making previous methods of rapid communication obsolete.

In addition, the entire Pony Express was apparently a financial disaster. Original costs were $5 per ounce. Later this was cut to $1 per ounce in an effort to stimulate greater use, but the Express never became a paying proposition to the owners.

Still, the effort represents a thrilling saga in our history, and a testimonial to the fortitude of young Americans. And while postage was a bit more expensive in the Pony Express era, it was apparently about as fast and reliable as present methods.

Nostalgia Ain't What It Was

Black Jack

A 1976 Associated Press news item which drew little attention told of the death of a horse. He was Black Jack, last of the Quartermaster-issued Army horses, and last to wear the U.S. brand. The big black Thoroughbred was 29, which in human terms would be more than a hundred years of age.

Black Jack was a ceremonial animal, used only for funeral processions, and never ridden. He was, according to military terminology, a "caparisoned" horse, a job he held more than twenty years. His ceremonial function was to be led, riderless, in the funeral procession, his empty saddle symbolizing the fallen warrior.

The exact origins of this custom go back into dim tradition. Primitive peoples throughout the world have always made an effort to honor the dead in such a way as to prepare them for success in the after-life. Consequently, food, clothing, weapons, and sometimes the wives or slaves of a mighty leader were buried with him. After all, he must be properly attended in the next world.

The warrior must also be furnished with appropriate transportation in the after-life, as well. Therefore, it was only logical to send his favorite horses along. The funeral procession would wind its way among the mourners, with the body of the fallen chieftain borne in state, but also in places of honor the assorted objects to be buried with him. According to the particular culture, the wives or slaves to be killed or buried alive might hold places of honor. The chieftain's horse would be led, riderless, to the burial site, where it would be killed on the grave.

Funeral customs have modified somewhat. We still honor the dead with the ceremonial procession, in the case of formal military or state funerals. However, the honor guard is not expected to accompany the fallen leader all the way to the hereafter. Likewise, the symbolic horse of the leader is no longer destroyed.

Black Jack served his function hundreds of times for cere-

113

monial funerals. Some of the recipients of his solemn services have been the high and the mighty, but others have been of humble station. The one common factor is that their lives were devoted to the service of their country. The horse was used in the funerals of Presidents Hoover and Johnson, and in that of General Douglas MacArthur.

Perhaps his most famous appearance occurred on November 24, 1963. The body of President John F. Kennedy was borne from the White House to the Capitol to lie in state. The military caisson with the casket was drawn by seven gray horses. These horses were three pairs, with a single leader. They wore standard artillery harness, with the left leader wearing a McClellan artillery saddle.

Just behind the caisson came the caparisoned horse, Black Jack, led by a soldier in dress uniform. The saddle was empty, and in the stirrups stood an empty pair of military boots, facing backward. A ceremonial sword in a silver scabbard swung from the pommel. Millions of people throughout the world saw the shiny black horse with a white star on his forehead dance proudly down the street, honoring the fallen Commander in Chief.

Now Black Jack is dead, having succumbed to the ravages of time. There will be a commemorative plaque at Arlington, but no ceremony was held. There will be memories, however, of a horse whose solemn duty during most of his life was devoted to the symbolic function of serving fallen warriors in the next world.

Nostalgia Ain't What It Was

Sidesaddle

Girls and horses seem to go together. At least, they do in our family. Maybe that's just because we've had so many of both around, but I don't think so. Teenage girls are one of the largest groups of buyers in the western stores, tack shops, and even in subscriptions to the horse magazines.

It seems perfectly logical to see large numbers of female entries in the horse shows. It should be noted that these entries aren't only in queen contests and pleasure events, either, but in barrel racing, poles, cutting, trail competition, and even roping. Tough endurance races around the country have many women entries.

There are a number of very capable women who are professional trainers. I know there are some people who will say that girls don't have the sheer physical strength to be horse trainers, but I don't believe it. Most men aren't as strong as a horse, either. Training is a matter of finesse, timing, and know-how, not just brute strength and awkwardness, anyway.

We also see a number of girl jockeys in recent years. This is logical. A girl is of more appropriate weight than most men. She has the sensitive nature to feel the horse's mood and to respond to it. Besides, a woman is built a little differently than a man, her weight distributed perhaps better to balance gracefully and efficiently on a horse. In general, I think women make excellent horsemen (horsepersons?). Most people consider girls and horses a good combination.

Alas, it was not always so! Man domesticated the horse many thousands of years ago, but even then it took him many centuries to learn to ride it instead of eat it. Even later came the idea of saddles. Eventually someone came upon the idea that maybe a woman (a useful item) might be carried on a horse (another useful item). Consequently, complicated platforms were constructed behind the saddle, with a board on which she could rest her feet (both on the same side, of course). Even after saddles for women became common, they were always expected to sit facing sideways, with feet on the aforesaid board.

115

About the seventeenth century, the idea evolved that a woman might possibly be able to sit facing forward, with her left foot in a stirrup, if she hooked her right knee around a saddle horn on the side of the saddle, near the front. This couldn't have been very comfortable, but apparently a lot of girls even participated in fox hunts and jumped fences with this crazy contraption. Undoubtedly there were some of the gals who protested, and some that even tried the more conventional saddles, but public sense of propriety kept the sidesaddle alive for centuries. Nicetas, the Byzantine historian, wrote that a woman who would ride with a leg on either side of a horse was a person of questionable moral character.

A friend of ours, a young woman who is an excellent horseman, once borrowed a sidesaddle to ride in a centennial parade. She practiced many hours in the sidesaddle to get both her horse and herself ready for the parade. Unfortunately, when the day came, the horse refused to let her mount! It wasn't the sidesaddle, however, but the full riding skirt and frilly hat that was causing the trouble. The horse was used to jeans!

Eventually the horse won out, and the disgruntled girl used the sidesaddle, but rode in her jeans instead of the riding skirt.

I don't know when it became ladylike to ride astride, but it's fairly recently. There are a lot of old sidesaddles still around that were used within the memory of people still living.

Lady Godiva's famous ride (about 1000 AD) must have been on a sidesaddle. Can you imagine the saddle sores she could get from one of those things?

Nostalgia Ain't What It Was

The Sole Survivor

I spent a year once as a student at the University of Kansas at Lawrence. One of the things I like to do when I have a bit of time in any area is to visit their museums. Consequently, I would occasionally while away an hour or so at the Dyche Museum.

One of the prominent displays was that of a stuffed horse. The animal wears a Seventh Cavalry saddle and blanket. He is Comanche, the horse ridden by Captain Miles Keogh at the Little Big Horn.

A placard stated that "Comanche was the sole survivor of the Custer Massacre", etc. I always thought that was a bit amusing. There were obviously large numbers of "survivors" on the other side. But back to the beginning.

The horse that was to be known as Comanche was bought by the army among a group of wild horses from the panhandle in 1868. He was thought to be about six years old, and the mustangers received $90 for him. He was branded with a US on the left shoulder, and assigned to Captain Miles Keogh of the Seventh Cavalry, in central Kansas. Keogh may have purchased the horse at cost from the government, as officers were required to furnish their own mounts.

At any rate, within a few weeks the Captain was riding the horse in the field. In a skirmish in September, an Indian arrow struck the animal in the right hip. A trooper who saw the arrow strike later said the horse "yelled like a Comanche." From then on he was "Comanche."

This was not to be Comanche's last battle wound. In 1870 and again in 1873, he received minor injuries in combat.

1876 found the Seventh committed against the largest concentration of Indians ever assembled. They met at a place called Greasy Grass by the inhabitants and Little Big Horn by the invaders. The result is history.

Indian sources say that Custer may have been among the first to fall. There are stories of a black-mustachioed officer, probably Keogh, who took command, riding back and forth to

Horsin' Around Again

attempt to bring together the shattered remnants of the column.

When the burial party reached the area two days later, Comanche was the only living creature on the field. He carried seven wounds and had apparently been considered too badly injured to be worth taking as part of the spoils.

Remarkably, perhaps, the burial party administered to the horse and actually led him fifteen miles to the steamer "Far West." The rescue boat would carry the wounded from Major Reno's command to Fort Lincoln, nearly a thousand miles away, in 54 hours. A place was made for the severely wounded horse. Too weak to stand or walk, he was placed in a sling and nursed back to health.

He was never ridden after 1878, but appeared at all parade functions of the Seventh, saddled and bridled, and draped in mourning. He became a mascot and a great pet of the troopers.

Comanche died at Fort Riley, Kansas in 1891 at the age of 29. Officers of the Seventh Cavalry wanted to preserve the remains, so L. L. Dyche of the University of Kansas was persuaded to undertake the taxidermy involved. The price agreed on was $400, but Dyche apparently agreed to waive the fee if the horse were left in the museum at KU.

Comanche still stands in Dyche Museum, now in a humidity-controlled glass case. There is a new placard. It begins:

"Comanche stands here as a symbol of the conflict between the United States Army and the Indian tribes of the Great Plains. . . ."

That's more like it.

Nostalgia Ain't What It Was

The Left Hind Quarter

We were in a delightful restaurant beside the highway, out in the heart of cattle country. It was before the dry weather, and the Flint Hills were green and lush. The view across the range land was beautiful. Our friends had invited us to this unique and attractive eating place.

The menu was unique, too. A rather extensive bill of fare for an out-of-the-way country inn. I was looking at the variety of sea food, but figuring I really ought to have beef out of deference to the cattleman we were with. I really enjoy it more, anyway. One of the ladies suddenly pointed to the menu.

"Well, what in the world does this mean?" She indicated a note regarding sugar-cured ham steaks. An asterisk beside the list referred to a footnote.

"Notice!" the menu proclaimed. "We serve only ham steaks from the left hindquarter."

That expression took me back a long way. It's probably been forty years since I heard a discussion of the left hindquarter. At that time the authority on such things (on most things, actually) was my grandfather Willett. He had come to Kansas in the 1860's in a covered wagon. His tales of buffalo and Indians and the prairie (he always said "prayer-ah") were heady wine for the palate of a youngster. He could always be relied on for stories of the "Olden Days." I've often wished we'd had a few more years with him. With a little more maturity, I'm sure I'd have gotten a lot more out of the stories.

At any rate, some of my favorite stories, as a small boy, were about some of his hunting experiences. Hunting, for many of his contemporaries, wasn't so much for recreation as for provisions. A group of neighbors would organize a deer hunt to furnish groceries for the families. The meat would be shared, but the unwritten rules provided that the person who made the actual kill received the skin and his choice of the meat. "First choice o' meat an' hide" was the way my grandpa always said it.

"Of course," he continued, "we'd always take the left hindquarter."

119

"Why, Grandpa?"

"Well, because it's the *best*, boy!"

"Why is it the best?"

That's about the closest I ever remember to a breakdown in communication with my grandfather. He pushed his hat back on his head and scratched his scalp. In retrospect, I can imagine his frustration.

"Jest because it is," he pondered. "I dunno — maybe because it's closer to the heart, and it gets better circulation. But it *is* the best."

Well, that was good enough for me. If he said it, it was gospel, at that time. And in the almost half century since, I've found very few things that he gave me a bum steer on (no pun intended).

I've never heard any explanation that I thought came any closer. I have heard old-timers seriously state that the left hindquarter is more tender, more juicy, finer grained, and so on. But usually no theory as to *why*. That was just a thing that everybody knew to be true. It's a lot harder to tell now, when it's all pre-packaged anyway, and you can't tell which hindquarter it's from. And a lot of our meat consists of both hindquarters ground up with everything else and served on a bun.

Incidentally, I heard an interesting set of figures recently. The largest trail drive ever to come up the Chisholm trail from Texas included 2300 steers. The trip would have been a tough one, of several weeks, with a lot of lonesome, weary days on horseback for the trail hands. But what a sense of accomplishment for the trail crew to arrive at their destination and deliver the cattle to the railhead. The drive might require the better part of a year of their lives in the planning and execution.

Now comes the astonishing figure. That entire herd, says the Chamber of Commerce, could be processed today by the local Iowa Beef plant *in just nine hours*! That's real progress but somehow a little bit sad. It makes me feel better to run into somebody like the people at the little country inn, who appreciate the finer things in life.

Like the left hindquarter.

Nostalgia Ain't What It Was

When the Work's All Done

When I was a pretty small boy, it was my privilege to spend part of the summers at an uncle's farm. That's where, I suppose, I got a lot of my interest in horses and livestock. All the field work was done with horses. I was a little too small to drive the work teams, but I'd get to ride them in from the field sometimes and help with things like shocking oats behind the binder. I'll bet I could still build a solid shock of oats.

But there was a little time to explore the pasture and the creek. We weren't supposed to go to the creek alone, but my brother and I had been close enough to see that there were a couple of interesting looking fishing holes. We were sort of short on male relatives who were fishermen, so were consequently a little short on fishing. We asked my uncle if he'd take us fishing some time.

"Sure!" he agreed. "We'll go, sometime when the work's all done."

It was a long time — maybe a couple of years or more, before I figured out that around a farm or ranch, the work's *never* all done. There is always fence to fix, weeds to cut, snow to shovel, stalls to clean, and so on.

I tried this same dodge on my own kids — putting them off "till the work's all done." Somehow, it seems to me that they caught on a lot quicker than I had. However, it has become a family joke — "some day when the work's all done."

There's an old folk song with the same theme: "When the Work's All Done This Fall." Apparently this is a universal problem. We always look forward to when school starts, or when school gets out, or after Christmas, or when things get back to normal. Whatever that is. These are all ways of saying the same thing: when the work's all done. Even Scarlett O'Hara in *Gone With th*e *Wind* had her way of saying it: "I'll think about that tomorrow."

I always feel sorry for the occasional retiree that I see with nothing to do. He'll work his whole lifetime looking forward to

121

retirement, and then be completely lost. Often he's so frustrated that his health will start to deteriorate almost immediately. He half-heartedly builds a couple of bird houses and then just sort of dries up.

I doubt if that's likely to happen to me. I've often thought that I could have retired at any time in the last twenty years, and spent the rest of my life just finishing things I've already started. I always have more things planned than I have time for, and books I want to read when I finish some of these other projects.

Speaking of finishing projects, we were visiting at the ranch of some friends a few years back. We were in their very attractive living room, a ranch style do-it-themselves project. We were talking horses, and I leaned comfortably back in front of the fireplace. Then I noticed that at the corner of the ceiling a strip of molding was missing. Our host saw me puzzling over it and answered my unasked question.

"That's where I didn't finish it," he observed.

Then he proceeded to tell me that his grandmother's people had very strong feelings about this. She was an American Indian, of what tribe I don't know. But part of her cherished beliefs included this: if a person ever *completely* finishes a project in every respect, that person will die! Maybe that's not too far-fetched. If you have something that you have to do yet, you want to be around to see it through. There's a saying that an old horseman never dies, he has to stick around to see how next year's colt crop looks. This in contrast to the early death of the retiree with nothing to do.

Now maybe if I can claim some Indian ancestry, I could have an excuse for all the unfinished projects I have. I'll think about that tomorrow, when the work's all done.

Nostalgia Ain't What It Was

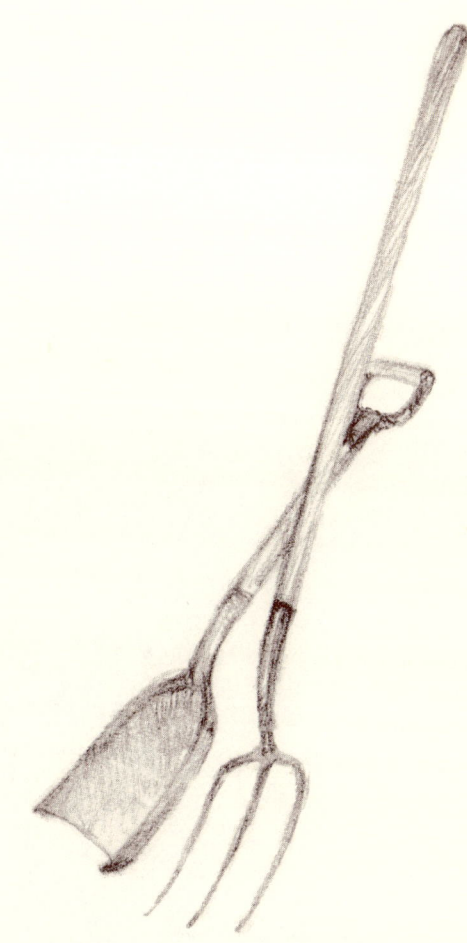

Animal Tales

Animal Tales

Wilful Disobedience

If you follow the horse-show circuits, or even if you just go to watch a horse show occasionally, you're probably aware of a competitive event called the Trail Class.

Originally, this started as an event to judge which horse would be best on the trail. The rider would have to open gates, take mail out of a rural mail box, drag a log or brush with a lariat, and such everyday activities. It was a pretty fair sample of a ranch horse's job.

In recent years, the Trail Class has, like other horse events, become more and more competitive. Each show committee likes to try to invent a trail obstacle that will surprise the horse and see how he reacts to it. Some of the old veteran show horses have seen about everything, so it's hard to surprise them. Some shows in recent years have featured courses that included an encounter with a rattlesnake, a cougar, an alligator, or an armadillo. Naturally, the dangerous items are caged or otherwise placed so there's no actual danger. Sometimes there will be fluttering streamers of crepe paper to walk through, or maybe a fuzzy pink chenille snake animated on a string. Nearly every Trail Class seems to include a wooden plank bridge and a black plastic tarp on the ground for the horse to walk across.

Of course, the horse which navigates all the obstacles without any hesitation whatever is going to be the winner. And that sometimes bothers me a little.

Do I really *want* a horse to ride that will do all that without any hesitation? True, it shows a lot of expert training and that the horse has a lot of faith and confidence in the trainer. But do I want a horse to just blunder along paying no attention to armadillos and fuzzy pink snakes? A rider in an actual trail situation will be better off on a horse that wants to take a minute to be really sure about it.

Many a cowboy has been kept out of trouble when his horse refused to do as ordered because the horse knew there was danger involved. This is called, by the animal behaviorists, "wilful disobedience." It involves a certain amount of judgement on the part of the animal, so a more intelligent animal is more likely to behave this way. That's why, in general, a smarter horse is a safer horse.

I understand the quality of wilful disobedience is highly desirable in guide dogs for the blind. We can easily imagine a situation where the blind owner tells the dog to cross the street, and the dog must refuse to obey because the traffic light is wrong. That's the whole idea of the guide dog — to act on information not available to the master. Mules have a reputation for being stubborn. Maybe justified, maybe not. But maybe a lot of the stubborn of a mule is wilful disobedience. In the mule artillery in the army, we were taught that if a mule is acting stubborn, there's a reason. Before you do anything, said our old sergeant, look for his reason.

One dark night we were on maneuvers in the Wichita Mountains. It was drizzling rain, and we couldn't see a thing. We were leading our train of pack mules along a trail on the shoulder of the mountain. Each man was holding the tail of the mule ahead, because we sure couldn't see where to follow. On our right was the face of the mountain, and on the left a sheer drop-off, we couldn't tell how far. A total blackout was in effect.

Suddenly, one of the gun mules up ahead balked. His driver pulled, pushed, and swore but the mule wouldn't budge. Word passed down the line, and one of the noncoms felt his way back with a shielded lantern to check on the problem.

The top-heavy gun load had shifted. Now the howitzer barrel, instead of on top, was jutting out to the right. If the mule had moved forward three or four feet, his load would have come into contact with the face of the mountain. That would have crowded the animal to the left, off the narrow trail, very possibly taking driver and packer with him over the cliff.

I can put up with a little wilful disobedience.

Animal Tales

The Trophy Hunter

Spot isn't a horse, he's a dog. A Dalmatian.

Spot became a member of our family several years ago. We had just lost our previous dog, Sherman, an Irish setter. Sherman had been such a favorite that we decided on an entirely different breed. A friend conveniently had a litter of Dalmatians and convinced us that a spotted dog would go well with our spotted horses. So Spot came home with us.

We've been accused of naming Spot in a hurry because we were late for 4-H meeting. Actually, we were just calling the fat little puppy "Spot" until we decided on a name, and we never got around to it. He just stayed "Spot."

Right away the puppy began to show a distinct personality. He decided that Mom was his person. She wasn't the one who fed him, even, but she was *his*. He's still jealous of her when the rest of us are around. He also decided he was one of the kids, although he was a kid that wasn't allowed in the house. He's only been in the house twice. Once was during a tornado that slashed a path of destruction just half a mile from us. The other time was during the wedding reception of our daughter April. Large numbers of people were coming in, and Spot did too, to see what was going on. Both times he was the one who decided when to come in and when to go back out. He behaved perfectly.

When anyone tries to take a picture, Spot is in it. We first noticed this when taking identification photos for registering horses. Nearly every attempt showed a grinning Dalmatian somewhere in the picture. I'm sure that the Appaloosa Horse Club thinks we have dozens of spotted dogs.

Spot's trophies are a long-standing family joke. When he was just a pup, he caught a rabbit one time. I think he was pretty surprised. He brought it up to the back door. Maybe he wanted to give it to Mom for a present, but mostly it seemed like he just wanted to keep it around for a souvenir. He was sort of proud of it. Didn't try to eat it, just kept it. He was a little upset with me when I hauled it off, but it was getting pretty fragrant.

One cold winter day a new stainless steel mixing bowl ap-

129

peared in place of Spot's feed pan. No one in the family knew anything about it. Spot seemed so proud of it that we eventually realized that he must have brought it for a trophy, like the rabbit. It was pretty, and shiny, and the dog plainly expected to be fed in it. We phoned around, but none of our neighbors seemed to be missing a mixing bowl. We decided to use it to feed the cats.

Within a few days the disappointed Spot had turned up with *another* stainless steel bowl! It appeared he was collecting the entire set. We let him keep that one for his own feed pan, until several months later. A neighbor from a quarter-mile up the hill discovered what had happened to her expensive mixing bowls and took them home. Spot sure didn't understand.

His latest trophy hunt involves a cow. There's a big pasture across the road where, at various times of the year, cattle are moved in and out, maybe forty or fifty steers or brood cows at a time. In a cattle operation of this sort, there are always some losses by death. Apparently, in some hidden gully, there's a long-dead steer. I'm sure of this, because Spot is bringing us trophies.

I don't know how he can even carry some of them. So far, he's brought three well-decomposed legs, a piece of rawhide about three feet square and, most recently, the skull. We think he's trying to build us a cow.

A Dog's Best Friend

W. C. Fields once made a remark to the effect that any man who dislikes children can't be all bad. Probably everybody, even those of us who basically feel the opposite, have had times when we could see his point. I have also heard this quote from Fields as "dogs and children", and I don't know which he actually said.

There's also the age-old truism that expresses a different sentiment, to wit, you can always trust a person that dogs like.

Animal Tales

That bit of sentimentality gives us a nice warm feeling, but I don't know how reliable it might be. I've known some pretty shifty characters with loyal dogs, and likewise, some relatively nice people, including myself, who have suffered dog bites.

It's true, however, dogs do seem to completely trust some people. Some guys can charm the meanest junkyard-type dog into a playful puppy. On the other hand, dogs dislike some people. Maybe it's a person's disposition, or his thought waves. I've often heard it said that dogs can tell if someone is afraid. I'm sure that's true. I'm somewhat afraid of dogs, from the time I was knocked down and mauled around by a playful big dog when I was about two years old. And I've always felt that dogs know this about me. That is, that they know that I'm afraid and distrustful.

Horses, too, seem to trust some people, and to be able to sense lack of confidence in a rider. I'm sure there's a great deal more communication on an unspoken level than we have any idea. That, of course, is why some people are highly successful as trainers. Horses instinctively trust them and understand their instructions. Other people are irritable and impatient, and their personalities simply don't lend themselves well to working with animals. They'll just never have it, and the animals know it. It's not a matter of experience, either.

A few years back, a young teenage girl was going to help us out with chores for awhile, and I was showing her the routine. She was very much interested in horses, but completely inexperienced. We had a yearling colt in the corral who didn't like to be handled. He was wearing a halter, but it usually took two or three of us to corner him and get a lead rope on him.

I was getting ready to explain all this, and that I didn't really expect her to catch and handle the colt, just to see that he was fed and watered. About then, I glanced around just in time to see the girl walk up to this half-wild colt and snap a rope onto his halter, while he stood perfectly calm. I guess the horse was reading her better than I was.

Of course, there are extraneous factors, too. Some time ago my wife was talking to a friend whose husband had run for local office. He had successfully survived the primary election, and Edna said we weren't surprised, because he's a man everybody likes.

"Well, maybe," remarked his wife, laughing, "but their dogs don't like him!"

Why not? Can't he be trusted? Of course, but the dogs' judgement is impaired. This man impresses the dogs with frightening scents, other animals, strange smelling chemicals, blood, and the memories of painful inoculations. You see, he's a veterinarian.

The Passing of Ten Point

In 1978, CBS carried a brief TV news film of a funeral. The unusual thing was that it was a funeral for a horse. A Japanese race horse.

The Japanese have a very special regard for horses, as I noticed when I spent some time in that country. They have numerous ancient legends and stories involving horses. In some of these, the horse is a supernatural being. But a *funeral* for one?

Of course, this wasn't just any old horse. He was Ten Point, a famous race horse. And the Japanese take their horse racing seriously. A favorite race horse in Japan will quite often have a fan club. Groupies hang around the paddock, bring flowers, and write fan letters. The horse owners and the track promoters seem to encourage this activity. After all, it's good for business.

In the TV news item they didn't give much information, just film of part of the funeral ceremony. I tried several standard sources of information to learn a little more, but struck out. Finally I wrote a hasty note to my sister who lives in Tokyo, and she answered right away with the information I was after.

Ten Point was a five-year-old race horse who had become a national favorite. I'm not using his name in translation. The

Animal Tales

Japanese called him Ten Point. Apparently a great many race horses in Japan are given English names. He had been entered in 18 races, and had won 11 of them. That may not seem like a terrific record, but two of the races were the Emperor's Cup and the Arima Memorial, the two biggest races in Japan. This makes Ten Point about like a Triple Crown winner in our country.

Ten Point fan clubs blossomed, and a great future seemed ensured. After all, 1978 — the Year of the Horse — would be only his third racing season. He had already earned 328 million yen — about a million and a half dollars. Plans were in the offing for sending Ten Point to race in France and later the United States.

Then, on January 22, 1978 in the ancient city of Kyoto, Ten Point's career came to an end. He was winning his race, when suddenly he broke stride and fell behind, limping badly. Examination of the animal revealed the right hind leg broken at the hock. Because of his fame, and probably because of his breeding potential, a valiant attempt was made to save Ten Point. A team of surgeons operated, and the horse was placed in intensive care. He appeared to do well initially, but after several weeks developed complications and died rather suddenly on Sunday, March 5.

The funeral was held at the Ritto Training Center near Shiga. Over 800 mourners were present, a capacity crowd in the meeting room. Hisamai Tokada, the owner of the horse, spoke "words of farewell"; one woman mourner read a poem (a time-honored Japanese custom at such occasions). Five priests participated in the ceremony, conducting a funeral ritual. Foremost among these was Enryu Oichi of Myoko-in Temple in Kyoto. (I'm not certain, but I believe this to have been a Shinto religious ceremony.)

Ten Point was buried at Yoshida Meadows on Hokkaido, the northernmost island of Japan. This is a traditional horse breeding area.

My sister called my attention to one other item. The news reports mention that Ten Point was "buried." If this is really accurate, it's pretty astonishing. No one, human or animal, is "buried" in Japan. Because of limited space, cremation became standard centuries ago. There are only a few exceptions: emperors and members of the immediate royal family are allotted space for burial. I've never been able to verify this, but if Ten Point was really "buried", that would be about the highest honor that could have been bestowed on a great horse.

The Baby-Sitter Cow

This past summer, after the hay was cut, we had a series of summer rains that made the grass come back lush and green. I had every available horse and colt — even Mildred, the old donkey — up in our 80-acre hay pasture to fatten and grow.

It began to look like there was more than enough grass even for that many animals, so I was sort of wondering about putting a few calves in there for a while. I don't know much about cows but I figured why not utilize this grass crop while we had it. We might not be so lucky another year.

I arranged a trade with a friend who has cattle. Some of my extra hay for three of his extra calves. Part of the deal was that we'd put these calves and their mothers on our grass till November, and then take the mothers out, leaving the calves. I still didn't have any actual cash tied up in this project, so figured I'd come out all right. I was getting a little static from my family but the calves were growing and getting fat.

Then somebody suggested that if there was an old cow in the pasture at weaning time it would be a big advantage. This is how I get myself into complicated situations sometimes, taking good advice. But it seemed reasonable. The newly-weaned calves would follow the old cow as a baby-sitter instead of running the fence and bawling, trying to find their mamas. This works pretty well with weanling horses, anyway.

Another friend had some whiteface cows with small calves that were about ready to go to the sale barn. I worked out a deal

Animal Tales

for one of these old cows and her three-month calf, not big enough to wean yet. The corralling and loading of this old cow and her calf was a tale in itself, but we did get them in my trailer, and I took them past the vet's to be properly blood tested, checked over, and inoculated for various diseases.

Then we headed for the home pasture, where the three cows and my calves were getting fat. I drove up pretty close to the cows and opened the back of the trailer. I expected the baby-sitter to join the others, but she took off at a fast gallop over the hill in the opposite direction. Her calf was right behind her, both their tails sticking up like flagpoles. The other cows just stopped chewing and watched in astonishment.

It was rainy that afternoon, but I went out again to check on the new cow and calf. I couldn't find them, but figured they were somewhere around, and it was getting dark so I went home. Next day was a Sunday, so Connie went with me and we spent an hour or two driving the pickup all over that 80 acres looking for the baby-sitter. She just wasn't there. We decided that she and her calf must have gone over, under, or through the fence at the north end and joined another herd of cattle up that direction. We alerted a couple of neighbors to keep an eye out for her, but nobody had seen her.

Next morning I went out to drive the country roads in the area, making mental plans to bring a couple of saddle horses out later. Maybe Connie and I could ride around the area and spot the missing animal. But as I passed our pasture, there they were! Baby-sitter and her calf, happily grazing with the others. Apparently she had hidden in some brushy draw for three days. She had finally decided there were no more shots and blood tests forthcoming and came out to join the others. Protective maternal instincts certainly run strong.

The Reasoning Process

Horsin' Around Again

It used to be said that the difference between man and the "lower" animals was the ability to think and reason. Then a few years ago, an English girl named Jane Goodall spent a lot of time watching wild chimpanzees. She recorded some pretty amazing observations.

For one thing, the chimps would make and use "tools." She repeatedly saw them strip bark and leaves from a stick and use the stick to poke into an ant hill or termite nest. Sometimes they'd even save the stick to use later.

Again, a young chimp saw a banana in an inconspicuous place. He didn't grab it, however. If he had, the bigger animals would have taken it away from him. Instead, he acted nonchalant and disinterested until he had a chance to sneak off with the banana. This sort of response, "deferred pleasure", is considered very advanced by the psychologists. Young humans don't achieve it for several years.

Animals don't think? We have to concede that either (1) maybe they do, or (2) maybe we have to change our definition of "human."

Of course, all animal lovers know that animals *do* think. Everyone has favorite examples, sometimes many of them. Some of mine have to do with horses, some with dogs and cats. Old Spot, for instance, before he lost his eyesight, would fight a buzz saw if I was around. Bigger dogs, coyotes, anything. Now this is a dog that's basically pretty chicken and doesn't like to fight. But if he knew I was around to bail him out, he was ready to go.

Interestingly, I never had to help him out in a fight except once. That time he was getting ready to pitch into a dog twice his size. I hollered to call him off, figuring the other dog would maybe chaw us both up. For a miracle, Spot stopped in mid-charge, the first time I hollered. That alone was a real rarity. I've always had a sneaking hunch that he had this whole thing figured out. He was counting on me to call him off *before* the donnybrook started.

Spot's look over his shoulder at the big dog, as he walked off said very plainly, "Boy, I'd cut you up in pieces if the boss hadn't stopped me!"

All of this was recently brought to mind by a friend telling me about a team of "work horses" back on the farm. They were full brother and sister. After a few years of good steady work in the fields, Buss, the gelding, became suddenly blind. "Moon-blind", it was called. I understand that the exact causes are still not well known.

Now, what good is a blind horse? Quite a bit, if he's a harness horse. His teammate can see, and the blind horse simply leans into the harness and follows along. He's as good at pulling as ever. In addition, the driver is guiding the team with the lines to indicate turns and all. They could continue to use the team.

The problem, in this case, would come when the horses were turned out to pasture. In the field were deeply eroded gullies, barbwire fences, and one narrow spot between a couple of outbuildings as they entered the gate. This could be pretty hazardous to a blind horse. A couple of the gullies were deep enough for a horse to fall into and break a leg or a neck.

It was Pearl, the mare, who came to the rescue and solved the problem. She apparently sensed the handicap of her teammate and seemed determined to take care of him. When a work team is at leisure, they usually graze side by side, like they work, but it soon became apparent that Pearl would change sides constantly. She was always between Buss and the hazard, the fence, gully, or whatever. He could even run and buck. She'd bump him gently with her shoulder if he made a wrong move and crowd him away from danger.

This mare actually was able to be the eyes of her blind teammate and keep the pair actively working for another ten years. Does anybody really want to argue that animals can't think and reason?

One of the Family

You may remember Stormy. We bought her nearly twenty years ago, for our daughter April, who was ten. The horse was a three-year-old filly, a beautiful coppery sorrel color, and with a marvelous gentle disposition. She has been part of our family ever since, until her sudden death recently from kidney disease.

Stormy could be stubborn and opinionated, but always seemed aware of her responsibilities to her rider. The mare helped raise a lot of kids, and we were always confident that she'd take care of them. She could respond to anyone from a very small child to a novice horseman to an expert, and handle any of these jobs efficiently. In her entire lifetime, not one person was ever injured while under Stormy's care.

She participated in a wide variety of activities, too. The mare was not only the first horse many people ever rode, but a 4-H project several times. She was the mare that sort of got us back in the horse business.

Stormy carried Joshua Lewis, the child actor, who was in our area to work on a movie, and joined our saddle club for a Veteran's Day parade. One of the major horse magazines carried a story about that event.

In 1976, my wife rode Stormy in the Bicentennial Wagon Train Pilgrimage for a day on the Santa Fe Trail. This was the only horse Edna has ever felt completely secure with. I know how she feels. Stormy was the first one I could muster the nerve to climb aboard after the horseback accident that broke my back sixteen years ago.

Innumerable trail rides, saddle club playdays, and shodeos, all were included in Stormy's career.

Along the line, she was also a mother. Stormy has presented us with a variety of foals, six or seven, I think. All were smart, good-looking animals, some of our best. Her most recent, a pretty filly named Sugar, is about six months old, with Stormy's personality.

One of Stormy's endearing characteristics was that whenever any of us came within her view, anywhere, anytime, she always called a greeting to us. No other horse has ever been so predictable about the morning "hello" when I step outside. Make no mistake about it, she was a member of the family.

A horseman once told me that he thinks it may be a mistake to get so attached to a horse that you wouldn't want to sell it. (I might take him more seriously if I didn't know how he feels about his old buckskin.)

Still, there are some advantages to this sort of close attachment. It hurts a little more to lose them, but you have a lot better memories. It's the reward of letting yourself love.

We don't do this with every horse. Of all we've ever owned, only a couple ever even approached how we felt about Stormy. It was tough to lose her unexpectedly but not as bad as if she'd had a prolonged wasting disease, with the eventual tough decision about having to put her to sleep. This way we have only the happy memories.

And there's other good stuff, too. When I went out this morning, Sugar raised her head and called the familiar greeting to me from the corral.

Dog Tales

Every time I manage to work a dog story into *Horsin' Around*, I always collect a bunch of retaliatory dog stories. I don't really intend to let things go to the dogs, so to speak, but some pretty good dog tales have turned up, so I'll pass them along.

I had mentioned that Spot and I have a sort of partnership in running our place. This prompted one hunter to tell me about his Brittany spaniel, Zip, who considered himself a full partner. The dog's owner and a friend were shooting ducks from a blind, and the dog was retrieving. The first duck was dutifully brought to the hunter, and the second to the friend. (Dogs *do* know who the bird belongs to.)

When the third duck hit the water, however, the dog seized it, swam to a sandbar in the lake, and buried the duck. He then returned happily to the blind.

Zip's owner was irate, but the friend nearly convulsed with laughter.

"He thinks that one's his!"

Apparently this was true. All day the dog impartially claimed every third duck and buried them on the sandbar. After all, a partnership should be share and share alike, right?

My brother once owned an Irish setter that was a whiz on quail. Old Red would hunt with us till we were ready to drop, and he'd still be eager to hunt. One time, however, on a beautiful November day, he found us a covey right in the middle of an open stubble field. The wind was right, the sun behind us, and the birds got up and flew directly away from us. Easy shooting. Except, we missed. Both of us, shooting double-barreled guns, missed with both barrels, and not a feather fell.

The dog turned slowly and looked at us in pure disgust. His tail drooped, and he trotted right past us and back to the car. We were completely unable to convince Red that he should give us another chance; he absolutely refused to hunt. We were finished for the day!

With increasing use of dogs to work cattle in our part of the country, I'm hearing more cow dog stories, too. There's an old rancher who's quoted as saying he's had to retire his best cow dog. The old dog is still getting around pretty well, and can still work the cattle as well as ever, but his eyesight is failing. He just can't read the brands any more.

An old uncle of my wife's told me this last story. He was the first man I ever saw really use dogs to good advantage in handling cattle. He started many years ago.

One time he was working a bunch of cattle across a brushy pasture to pen them. His dog put the cows into the brush and moved them on through in good shape. When they came out the other side a half mile away, however, there was one missing. He sent the dog back in. In a few minutes, the dog was back, whining, crawling, apologetic, but without the cow.

Normally his owner would have whipped the dog, but he says the dog already acted so remorseful that he just scolded him severely. Then he very firmly sent the animal back after the missing cow. The dog crept into the bushes, tail between hind legs, and disappeared. He did not return.

The owner waited for half an hour, increasingly irate. Finally he plunged into the brush himself, determined to not only find the cow but to teach the dog a lesson. He thrashed around for another quarter hour before he spotted the dog, lying quietly and cowering from the expected punishment.

However, the dog was lying near a jumbled pile of rocks. As he approached, the rancher noticed that it was the rim of a long-forgotten abandoned well. And about twenty feet down, at the bottom of the dry well shaft, was the missing cow, dead from a broken neck.

Blue Lightning

In some ways, cowboying hasn't changed a lot in the last hundred years. It's still a man on a horse, chasing cows, for the purpose of all the variety of things that make up a cattle operation — branding, ear marking, dehorning, doctoring, castrating, and so on.

Of course, a cowboy is a lot more mobile nowadays. He can cover a lot more country in a pickup truck than on horseback. He may do both, actually, pulling a trailer for the horse while he moves from one pasture to another. A man can check a lot more cattle than a few years ago.

He's got one other thing going for him now that few old time cowboys had. A great many ranchers have a good dog to work cattle. The first time I saw a cow dog work was over 20 years ago. The dog was a border collie, and he was used not on beef cattle, but on milk cows. I was visiting a pretty good-sized dairy operation, and they would send this dog out to bring the cows in from pasture. The dairymen could just sit in the shade while the dog went after the cows and put them in the stanchions. They did have to hook up the milkers and throw a little feed, but the dog was surely taking a lot of the leg work out of handling the dairy.

A time or two in the last few years I've seen cattle gathered, bunched, divided, and moved by cowboys without even a horse around. Just a couple of good working cow dogs. The dogs seem to instinctively know what's needed and handle a large bunch of stock with just a nip on the heel here and there.

You hear a lot of stories about somebody's smart blue heeler or whatever. Some of the prices being paid for well-trained stock dogs are really breathtaking. This is sort of like the price of horses. A horse isn't worth anything until somebody's ready to buy him. Then he's worth any amount the buyer is willing to part with.

All this reminds me of a dog story recently told me by Speck Mann. Speck knew an old rancher down in the brush country near Uvalde, Texas, where the mesquite, catclaw, cholla, and prickly pear make cowboying on horseback pretty tough. That's where chaps originated, as I recall.

Anyway, a cattle buyer from Fort Worth was commenting on the situation.

"I don't see how you can work cattle in this," he commented. The old rancher was quick to respond.

"We use cow dogs," he proclaimed. "I'll show you!"

The pickup lurched to a stop at a barbwire gate, and the active little dog jumped to the ground. He was ordered to "sit" while the rancher explained. The dog was to bring out one particular animal. A brocklefaced brindle cow with a crumpled horn. She'll have a 33 branded on the right shoulder, the dog was told, and a Lazy S brand on the left hip.

The dog started into the mesquite, but was called back and asked to sit again.

"Now be sure you got it!" instructed the owner. "Jest that one cow," and he repeated the description.

The dog plunged into the square mile or so of brush, and in a few minutes, crashing down the draw came a large animal. Out in the open, with the dog in hot pursuit, a brindle cow with a brockleface and a crumpled horn, and the proper brands!

The next time he was in Fort Worth, the rancher found that the cattle buyer had told everyone around the stockyards about the fantastically smart dog down at Uvalde.

"Is your dog really that smart?" someone asked.

"Well, he's purty smart, I guess," answered the cattleman modestly. "Reckon I forgot to mention, though, that was the onliest cow in that pasture."

Another man bought a rather expensive dog to work sheep in a mountain area. The dog was eager and willing, and was an expert at his job. On command, he would gather sheep from the rocky sagebrush hillsides and bunch them together.

The dog had one major fault, however. When he was "called in" by voice and arm signals, he would come immediately, instantly, and without regard to anything else. If there happened to be sheep in his path, Old Blue would charge right through, scattering and frightening the carefully-gathered sheep.

This became more and more irritating to the owner, and

finally he decided to sell the dog. He placed an ad in a carefully selected newspaper, far enough from home so that none of the readers would know the dog. Blue had already become a joke among the local stockmen.

A prospective buyer, a sheep rancher, answered the ad, was interested and agreed to come and look at the dog.

"But," he specified, "I want to see him work sheep."

The two ranchers drove out to an area where the dog's owner had two or three hundred sheep grazing, and Blue was released.

"Go get around 'em!" the owner called, with appropriate arm signal. The dog expertly dashed across the rocky hillside and through the brush, searching out stragglers, and in a remarkably short time had gathered the entire flock in a bunch on level ground, circling to keep them together.

The prospective buyer was certainly impressed, but the best was yet to come. The owner waited until the dog was exactly on the opposite side of the flock from the watching rancher.

"Okay, Blue," he hollered, with the arm signal to come in, "divide 'em in two!"

The Foster Mother

It's nice to have good neighbors. The neighbor across the road from our pasture north of town has certainly kept us out of a lot of trouble from time to time. It's nine miles from our house, and while we check on the livestock up there nearly every day, sometimes things happen when we're not around.

That's the way it was one Sunday morning this summer. The phone rang shortly after daylight, and my good neighbor reported strange happenings.

"Your donkey," he reported, "is chasing, or playing with, one of the baby calves. It can't get back to its mother."

Animal Tales

I dressed in a hurry and jumped in the pickup. On the way up there, I was expecting the worst. Donkeys are sometimes pretty aggressive toward a smaller animal. I'd seen this one, an old pet named Mildred, rush at a dog with very serious intent a time or two. We once found the remains of a young coyote in the pasture that I was certain had been Mildred's victim.

Now about all we needed was for the donkey to start attacking calves. Aside from the worrisome nature of the thing, a newborn calf was worth quite a little this year. I was a bit puzzled. There were several horses, as well as the handful of cows in that pasture, and none of them had ever bothered baby calves before.

When I drove in and shut the gate, I could see the little black white-faced calf curled on the ground, with Mildred standing over him. The calf's mama was standing a little way off, bawling to him. As I drove closer, the calf jumped up and ran toward his mother. Instantly, Mildred leaped between them, turning the calf like an expert cutting horse. The old cow approached, but the donkey turned and threatened her with ears back, and to my surprise, the cow backed off.

The tired calf went off a little way and lay down again, and Mildred stationed herself near by. My gosh, I finally realized, she's not trying to hurt it, she wants to adopt it! This seemed to be the case. The donkey was behaving exactly like a mother, protecting this calf from everything, including its own mother!

Mares with a strong mother instinct sometimes do steal a foal. We once had some friends whose mare stole another mare's foal this way. Unfortunately, she had no milk, and by the time they realized what was happening, the foal had starved.

And that was my fear in this case. Mildred was preventing the calf from nursing. The old cow's udder looked uncomfortably full.

I decided Mildred had to be moved. Now normally the old donkey would be rubbing up to me to be petted, and I'd put a halter on her. This time? No way. I couldn't catch her. I finally decided to rope her. My first throw missed. So did the second, but the rope whacked her hard across the ears. Mildred decided she didn't want that calf bad enough to fight me for it. She struck out at a lope for the other end of the pasture.

A grateful calf ran to his mother and started to chow down. Mildred hasn't bothered a calf since.

A Heck of a Nose

I have a friend who loves to go with me on my day off. I'm usually doing things like hauling feed or hay, or at any rate, doing outside things. Most of them require the use of the old pickup truck, and my friend loves to ride in the pickup. His name is Spot, and he's our old Dalmatian, the "trophy hunter."

Actually, Spot isn't really old, only ten or eleven. But he just had a sudden occurrence of glaucoma, and almost overnight his sight was gone. We took him up to the Veterinary School at Manhattan, and they checked him over completely. He was in fairly good general condition, but nothing could be done for his sight. Except for that, they told us, he should have a few good years ahead.

He was already showing signs of adapting rapidly. The blindness wasn't one of these partial things. Spot would literally run into the side of the barn. But he began to change his routine and depend more on his other senses.

Formerly, in his job of defending the premises from all harm, he'd make rounds every morning just after daybreak. A big circle around the house and outbuildings represented his perimeter. His circle went up through the pasture, down by the road, and back through the orchard, about 75 yards out, stopping at selected sign posts.

After his handicap, he tried to keep it up, but soon realized he couldn't handle it. It was downright dangerous to him to circle through the pasture. Horses could easily step on him. So he gave it up. He still makes his morning rounds, but has pulled his perimeter in to about 50 feet. That puts him entirely inside the yard, and is much easier for him to handle.

He also remembers where everything is located. If we have a feed bucket where it shouldn't be, or somebody parks a car in an unexpected place, Spot will often collide with it. That embarrasses him. Once he got confused crossing a footbridge with me at the north pasture. He panicked and just lay down on the bridge and cried till I "saved" him. But he tried it another time and now can navigate the bridge by feel. He only fell in the creek once while learning.

I don't know when he began to lose his hearing. I'm not sure whether he hears at all. Edna says he's like the kids used to be, and hears what he wants to, but I think he's nearly deaf.

Spot has developed a couple of his other senses to compensate for his losses. One is pretty hard to explain, a sort of ESP, I guess. I've always let him ride along with me when I'm going in the truck to the feed store, or to haul hay, or to check the pasture. Other times, I'm going places a dog can't go. Spot has always known which it is. If I'm going to town, he doesn't even bother to raise his head when I start the engine. If I'm headed for the pasture, he's waiting by the pickup for me to open the door. I used to think he could tell by the way I was dressed, but now it's got to be something else. And Edna says if I go off to the pasture or the feed store and leave Spot at home, he cries all the time I'm gone.

Spot's nose, though, is his most remarkable sense. He can sort out the most recent of a dozen crisscrossing tracks, and ground-trail me to wherever I'm out working. I said earlier that the old dog never gets further than 50 feet or so from the house, except when he's with me. Well, he did at least once.

There's a neighbor up the road about a half mile who has a beautiful long-haired English sheep dog. Imagine everyone's surprise when she turned up unexpectedly one day with a litter of spotted pups.

"I thought your old Spot was blind and deaf," her owner wondered.

Well, yes, he is; but he's got a heck of a nose.

The Settin' Hen

Horsin' Around Again

During the months of late summer, things around a farm home with kids hit a sort of frantic zenith. That's Fair time, and there are 4-H projects to finish, animals to groom, and all manner of desperate attempts to get ready for the Fair.

If there are kids in cooking projects, the family is dutifully eating all the failures and just as dutifully refraining from eating the successes, which are being carefully frozen to take to the Fair.

Sewing projects are spread over dining tables and living room floors. Any mere male who tries for a kiss as he starts out the door to work may have second thoughts. There is the ever-present danger of being perforated by the mouthful of pins worn by the females of the family at this season.

Fathers are pressed into service to assist in hauling various livestock to parades, arenas, and Fairgrounds. Sometimes in the bustle and confusion it's possible to overlook the routine and commonplace. Things like eating and sleeping, even. And how much easier to overlook the commonplace but unexpected. Like the settin' hen.

When we first moved to our present home about a dozen years ago, it was already an old farmstead. There were a few half-wild "banty" chickens around the old outbuildings. They have continued to thrive. Some years we've managed to harvest some of them, and we do use some of their eggs. At one time I intentionally "bred them up" by turning loose some Cornish roosters. This produced a bit heavier chicken, better for the table, and with slightly bigger eggs. They are a nuisance around the barn, but I sort of enjoy them. Besides, I don't think we *could* get rid of them. They're about as wild as pheasants. The hens hide their nests in the outbuildings or in the brush and weeds, and hatch more half-wild offspring — which brings us back to my story.

As Fair week approached it seemed that we were heading in six different directions with the horse trailer. There was a horse show at the saddle club arena, then two days later the parade downtown to open Fair week itself. This requires considerable in the way of planning and logistics, by the way, to drop off horses and riders at one end of the parade, and pick them up several miles away at the other end a couple of hours later.

Then the next day was when we'd be showing horses at the Fairgrounds. So another trip with the trailer, park it for the day at the Fair, and finally, late afternoon, home with the trailer. I pulled in, backed the big trailer into position, and climbed out to block the wheels and unhitch.

Meanwhile, Connie was unloading her horse.

"Hey, Dad," I heard her call from inside the trailer. "Did you know there's a hen in here?"

I walked around and stuck my head in the front door. Sure enough, there was a little brown hen on her clutch of eggs in one of the mangers at the front of the trailer.

A setting hen is pretty hard to dislodge. They will remain quiet until practically kicked off a nest if they think they aren't seen. I've seen some hens hide nests in pretty unusual places, but this really took the prize. This hen had been staying faithfully on her nest while the trailer had been hitched and unhitched several times. To different vehicles, even. She had been hauled around, we figured, over a hundred miles. We could just imagine her apprehension as we'd back the pickup in to hitch up.

"Oh, lordy, here we go again!"

We decided to leave her alone to see what would happen, and a couple of weeks later, it did. She hatched one lone chick. I suppose the rest of her eggs had been spoiled from the bumpy rides.

But boy, that one well-traveled survivor sure had something for "show and tell"!

Instinct or Understanding?

I wrote once before about an old mare we have whose mother instinct makes her a bit dangerous at foaling time. This mare is calm, friendly, easy-going, and a regular old pet. The first time she had a foal after we owned her, we were all anxious to see the baby, and the whole family crowded down to the barn to see.

She didn't seem to object as we stood and looked over her newborn, but after a few minutes of flash bulbs and conversation, she decided we had enough pictures and that she needed privacy. The mare charged at the group of us with teeth bared, knocked the pipe out of my mouth, and drew blood on one of the girls who was a trifle slow to move out. She has repeated that biting episode a couple of times through the years. Usually she gives just one good hard bite along the side of the bitee's neck or on the shoulder muscles.

Why would we want to keep an animal with this sort of disposition? Well, for one thing, that's *not* her disposition. She's really a gentle, friendly mare. It's just that she goes through this instinctive protection thing when she has a new colt. It lasts only a few days, and then she's a regular old pet again. She'll even let us handle her colt in a week or less. Any time we've ever been bitten, it was our fault, not hers, because we weren't respecting her instincts. Besides, she has had some very good colts for us, so it's worth while being a bit cautious for a few days when she foals.

It did get a bit hair-raising one time, I'll admit. A few years ago we had this mare in a small pasture near the house to foal. I knew she was pretty near to delivery, so we were checking on her night and morning. The weather was warm, and she would give birth outdoors in the clean grass.

One day, I came home just before dark and the weather was turning heavy and muggy, threatening to rain. Glancing down toward the mare, I could see her standing over a newborn foal, not even on its feet yet. She was on a narrow neck of land that jutted out into the creek, and the colt was clear out on the point. On three sides was a sheer drop of about four feet to the water.

Animal Tales

I began to worry about the baby. If it got up and floundered around as they usually do, it was sure to fall in the creek. To make matters worse, the stream usually floods over its banks when it rains, and it was starting to rain and to get dark. We *had* to get the foal out of there.

I changed clothes, pulled on a slicker, and recruited a couple of the older kids to get a lantern and help me. It was completely dark by this time, and when we approached we could see the mare standing across the narrow part of the neck of land, blocking access to the foal. It was raining harder. I didn't know what to expect, except that she had a history of some pretty aggressive behavior, but I figured we'd lose the colt if we didn't do something. It was still lying huddled on the ground.

The kids held the lantern while I slipped a halter on the mare, and then one of them held the lead rope while I eased past her toward the foal. None of us had been bitten yet. I knew if the mare charged me they couldn't hold her, so I was fully prepared to jump in the creek if I had to, to get away. I just hoped they'd holler soon enough to give me some warning if she started for me. I sure couldn't watch her.

I gathered up the shivering baby, a nice filly, and the mare watched me every second, "talking" softly to the foal. I carried it past her, and on up the hill to the barn, the mare contentedly following. She understood, apparently, that she had needed help.

I'd like to report that from then on she let us handle her foals, but this was just one exception. The next year she was as mean as ever!

Gatherin' Sunbeams

"Let's Pertyke"

When the kids were small I was half listening to their chatter one day while I did something else. They kept using a word that I didn't quite understand.

"*Pertyke* we're going to a horse show."

"*Pertyke* you have a new colt, and. . . ."

"This will be our *pertyke* corral. . . ."

I began to wonder if they had started to speak some foreign language without my knowledge. Finally I had to find out. I went in where they were playing on the floor, with dolls, horses, a corral made of boxes, and the entire Johnny West entourage of horse trailer, jeep, and all.

"What," I questioned, "is this *pertyke* thing you're doing?"

I got a couple of shocked stares. (Dad doesn't even know *that*?) They attempted to explain, and suddenly I saw the light. "Pertyke", I realized, wasn't a word at all, but a rapidly slurred form of a phrase.

"Let's-pretend-like" became usefully shortened and could be instantly inserted anywhere in play to set the stage for the upcoming events. It became a magical phrase to denote that this is our play today, which may easily be our serious endeavor tomorrow.

I once heard the remark that children's play is their work. It is used as a learning experience for later life. Playing house, playing school, or excavating in a sand box are all experimental attempts to try on the responsibilities of the adult. "Pertyking" is a very useful educational experience.

It occurs to me that young animals go through exactly the same process.

We were eating at the kitchen table the other day and watching the horses in the pasture behind the house. A couple of two-year-old geldings were cavorting and bucking. They paused right in front of our window, and both reared high on their hind legs, striking and biting at each other. Now when a fifteen-hand horse stands clear up on his hind legs he's pretty impressive. Here were two of them, ears back, and to all appearances acting like murderous wild stallions, intent on a fight to the death for possession of the mare band. The next instant they were off and running again, happily playful.

But I'm sure that for an instant, each horse was pretending that he was the Wild Stallion of the Rockies. These *pertyke* games enable the young animals to develop muscle and wind and stamina.

Anyone who has seen kittens play can easily see the mystique of *pertyke*. One kitten crouches down like a hunting tiger, and leaps from concealment on his apparently unsuspecting litter mate. They'll roll over in an apparent death struggle, developing skills that may be very useful in the future. A farm cat, especially, is learning hunting skills that will make him a good hunter, in addition to holding his own against coyotes, hawks, owls, and other predators.

Sometimes, I'm sure, animals *pertyke* just as children do, just for the fun of it. There is a small knoll about a hundred yards behind our house, one of the highest points in the pasture. It overlooks the pond and the barn. Many times I'll look out, and there will be one of the horses, carefully posed on the crest of the hill. The scene looks for all the world like a calendar painting of a wild horse. Head up, neck arching, ears alert, the horse is involved in some daydream fantasy for a little while.

Pertyke can be very useful, too. One summer a mother skunk raised a litter of six kittens under the back porch. As mother skunks do, she abandoned them when she thought they were old enough, so we had baby skunks wandering around the yard for a few days.

Now just a couple of weeks before, our old dog Spot had tangled with mama skunk. Right at the back screen door, in fact, but that's another story. Anyway, when the baby skunks came out, Spot would amble right past them, thoughtfully gazing off into the sky somewhere. He'd *pertyke* they weren't even there. (He sure didn't want a repeat of his adventure with Old Mama.)

Hunting Season

One of my favorite seasons is the fall. By this time winter has pretty well taken over, but I'm never quite ready for it. The autumn colors change so rapidly, different from day to day. The long, hazy, sunny days of October and November are a sort of invitation to get out and tramp around. Even people who aren't particularly outdoors-oriented thrill to the call of wild geese in the November sky. There's still just a bit of wanderlust in all of us.

The prairie is beautiful in autumn, too. Anyone who has not seen the Flint Hills in fall wardrobe can hardly appreciate it. The sea of green overnight turns gold and orange and red. It's worth being alive, just to get out occasionally.

I think that's the reason a lot of people hunt. It's an excuse to get out of town and enjoy the outdoors. I used to do quite a bit of hunting at one time, but have slowed down on it considerably in recent years. There are just too many other things to do, and I'm usually outdoors anyway.

Horses and hunting have deep roots together. Domestication of the horse made it easier for man to hunt. The American Indian built an entire culture around this fact. When the average American thinks of the Indian, the picture in his mind is of the *Plains* Indian, the buffalo hunter on horseback.

In the south, a lot of quail hunting is done on horseback. The hunters follow the bird dogs, and when a covey is pointed, they dismount to shoot. The National Field Trials for hunting dogs are conducted in this manner. In fact, there has evolved a type of saddle called a field trial saddle, originally for this purpose. It's a modified English saddle, as opposed to the western stock saddle. Actually it looks a lot like the European military saddles of the last century. I understand the field trial saddle is very popular in the endurance ride competitions.

No mention of hunting and horses would be complete without mention of Robert Doudican's Appaloosa gelding that could point quail. A number of people have seen him do it. Bob could never get him to retrieve, though.

One of the more famous of Indian scouts of an earlier day was a Kiowa called Tsain-Tonke. (There are several other spellings.) He is usually referred to as Hunting Horse or Hunts-a-horse. There seems to have been a little confusion as to whether he was named for a horse used for hunting, a buffalo horse, or whether it means "looking for a horse." I have been told by one of his descendents that he was called Hunts-a-horse because as a child he loved horses so much that he was always hanging around them, "hunting a horse." Seems logical. Incidentally, his family now use the spelling "Tsatoke", and translate it simply "Horse."

One final hunting story. A rancher friend tells of some city hunters who stopped at his place and asked permission to hunt prairie chicken. He directed them to the proper area and asked them to stop back and report their luck.

In due time they stopped at the house to report that they had gotten only one chicken.

"It sure is a nice one, though," said the city man, proudly displaying — a chicken hawk!

"Yep," said the rancher, not even changing his expression. "Sure is."

Now that's when he ends the story. But my favorite mental pictures are back in the city, the hunters trying to cook and eat that tough old hawk. I can just imagine them sitting at the table, telling each other, "By gosh, Joe, do you realize those idiots out there in the Flint Hills eat these things all the time?"

Gatherin' Sunbeams

The Classified Ads

Somebody recently called my attention to the fact that the classified ads in the horsemen's magazines have changed a lot in recent years. I took a look, and sure enough! Sprinkled through the "Miscellaneous" section will be things like:

"40-year-old bachelor ranch owner, no bad habits, wishes to meet attractive single woman between 35 and 45 who enjoys country life."

My gosh! What's next? Mail order brides? There was quite a bit of that in the early days. I know one old-timer who actually had a mail order bride. He'd paid her way from the old country. I knew the lady, and believe me, if ever a customer deserved a refund — but that's another story.

It's interesting to look at the personal columns sometimes. "I will no longer be responsible for the debts of Jane Doe, etc." I always think that's sort of a tragedy. I once saw a switch on that:

"I, John Doe, will continue to be responsible for the debts, care, comfort and well-being of Jane Doe as long as I may live." Now that probably embarrassed the lady, but I thought it was sort of sweet. I'll bet she did, too.

You can tell a lot sometimes about a person by his ad. Take one from the local paper a couple of years ago.

"Wanted to buy: riding lawn mower with self starter. Also, bicycle exerciser." There's a message there somewhere.

Of course, the ad doesn't always come out just like it's intended. A lady I heard of phoned to place an ad in her local paper to sell some Toulouse geese last fall. When the paper came she hurried to see how her ad came out. It took her a while to find it, and then she had to recognize it by the phone number.

"For sale: two loose skis . . . ."

I'll bet the advertising department had a hard time figuring why she'd wanted it in the "Livestock" section.

One of my all-time favorites I saw in a publication with national circulation a while back.

"For sale: pet alligator, four feet long. Gentle, will eat most

159

anything. Fond of children."

Hmm . . . .

Somewhat recent in scope is the tendency to express political opinions in the classified ads. I really think that's a sort of a waste. Nobody looks at it as soon as they see what it is. Of course, it's good for the paper, and keeps money in circulation, so I guess it's all for the good.

A reader recently sent me an ad clipped from a Colorado livestock paper which does much the same thing. It leaves no doubt where the advertiser stands.

"Agricultural opportunity for young couple to operate or purchase established farming operation on contract. Must have desire to be successful. Race, religion, and education unimportant. No long-haired Democrat union sympathizers need apply. Apply at . . . ."

You have to admit, it's timely. I still have the address if there's anybody who wants a crack at it.

The Gentle Art of Profanity

When I was a kid growing up, we weren't allowed to use profanity. This was a Methodist minister's home, and any form of vulgarity was really frowned on. We couldn't even say "heck" or "darn" or "gosh" because my mother insisted that those were rowdy words too. They were merely substitutes for words we were sure to be thinking. So no slang even. About the strongest we could get past my mother's censorship was "aw, fuzz!"

The strongest expletive I ever heard my ministerial father use was "oh, pshaw." Not that he didn't know the words. He grew up in the rough end of Joplin, Missouri, and well understood the proper use of strong language, preacher or not.

So I was a little unprepared for the situation I found in the army, in the mule artillery. We had an old Regular Army sergeant who was the most expert cusser I've ever heard cuss. I mean, it was a display of skill when Sarge put on an exhibition. You knew you were listening to a master in his field.

Part of his charm was that he never just dropped profanity around carelessly in normal conversation. It was reserved for special occasions. He was said to have once cussed a group of new recruits for three minutes straight without repeating himself. He'd cuss until he was out of wind, take a deep breath in mid-sentence, and continue. The deep breath was the only punctuation he indulged himself in.

And talk about colorful! Besides the occasional references to deity and the hereafter, the broad range of subjects involved in Sarge's repertoire was amazing. His profanity dealt with legitimacy, genealogy (especially maternal), circumstances and mode of his cussee's conception and upbringing, and a variety of sexual deviations. He was known to mention homosexuality, incest in several forms, bestiality involving innumerable species, and including mammalian, avian, and amphibian subjects. Various dietary preferences were discussed, along with a certain amount of descriptive material involving excretion. If you heard Sarge really unwind, you'd heard it all.

In the Pacific, we were in contact from time to time with various foreign troops. The Australians had more swearing ability than any of the other Allied troops we met. They went at it a little differently. Instead of Sarge's custom of letting it all pile up for use at a single session, the Aussies sprinkled just a bit at random through a conversation. Sort of like seasoning, I guess.

It sure was colorful. The average Aussie would think nothing of breaking a sentence or even a phrase to insert profanity. The more skillful could really spice up a visit. The ultimate was on an occasion when I actually heard a sergeant from Down Under break a *word* in the middle to insert profanity. Somebody else was talking and he wished to express total agreement with the speaker. His exclamation, while not exactly grammatical, leaves no doubt as to where he stood. "Abso-goddam-lutely!"

More recently I heard an expression by a local cowboy that,

under the circumstances, I consider a masterpiece. A mutual friend had come into possession of some pornographic literature. A lewd, crude, filthy sort of a picture magazine that left nothing to the imagination. He contrived to let his friend see it, more or less accidentally. The cowboy looked dubiously at the cover, then casually opened the magazine and saw the first of the really obscene photographs. His eyes widened, and out of his astonished mouth popped a superb expletive.

"Wal, shuckie-darn!"

Ghost Horses

> *"From ghoulies and ghosties*
> *And leggity beasties*
> *And things that go bump in the night*
> *Good Lord deliver us"*
>
> Old Scottish prayer

Apparently the human race has always had a fear of the dark and the supernatural. I suppose youngsters have always grown up scaring the daylights out of each other with ghost stories. And at this time of year, it's time again for ghosts and goblins and disembodied spirits to walk, fly, float, or whatever they do. A lot of good ghost stories, songs, and legends have to do with horses. There are a wealth of stories about ghost riders, ghost horses, and various such supernatural phenomena.

Why ghost horses? Why not cows, sheep, or other animals? Of course, black cats have a special place, so do bats, owls, and werewolves, but horses do hold a prominent place in stories of the supernatural. For instance, a bad dream is a "nightmare." Who ever heard of a "nightcow"?

A lot of famous writers, including Washington Irving and Edgar Allan Poe, have written stories involving supernatural horses. There are dozens of local legends of the west involving a wild ghost horse who, when chased by riders, escapes by simply disappearing.

Not too long ago, people firmly believed that elves occasionally steal a horse from its stall, ride it all over the country on some unknown devil's mischief, and then return it. The exhausted horse, with dried sweat and mud on its flanks, wasn't much good the next day, and that was the proof. Even further proof was to find a burr or two in the horse's mane or tail, picked up in some remote and weed-tangled place on the journey.

And did you know that elves tangle horses' manes? They also tangle extension cords, and twine in drawers, but really our forefathers actually attributed the tangles in a horse's long mane to elves.

In this part of the country, we usually clip a horse's mane, but horses which have flowing manes are plagued with a very curious tendency for the mane to tangle. The tangles involve a few strands of hair, perhaps a plait as thick as a pencil. Sometimes they are twisted so uniformly that they actually appear to be braided. In fact, I once suspected that my kids had braided three or four plaits in the mane of one of our brood mares. They indignantly denied it, but I really wasn't convinced.

I became convinced some time later, though. We have one brood mare who, before we bought her, was a range mare. She is wild as a deer and can't be caught without actually running her down and roping her. I was out looking over the mares, and there in her mane was a single three-strand plait, like a girl's braided pigtail! Now I know no one can even catch that mare, much less get her to stand still for that. Maybe it *is* elves!

The most spine-chilling of the supernatural horse stories is that of the Irish "pooka." Ireland is full of folktales, leprechauns, and fanciful creatures, but the pooka tops them all.

A pooka (also spelled puka, pukah, or pookah) is a supernatural being in an animal body. It could be any animal, but is usually a horse. It could be any horse, and may be a perfectly docile, useful animal, used for years by its master, and perhaps even a superior type of animal. It is usually highly intelligent, so is easily trained.

There is one catch in the story. A pooka horse, says the legend, is a water spirit, and he has a lifelong desire to return to the ocean. He will postpone this urge until just the right moment, when he is near a large body of water, lake, river, or ocean. Then he will plunge in, swimming strongly straight down to the bottom, carrying his hapless rider to a watery grave!

Wow! I've ridden some horses which had unpleasant habits, but this is ridiculous! It's enough to give you nightmares.

Mixed Team

A reader sent me a photograph recently of a very unusual cart and team. The picture was taken about 1943 or 1944, and shows a homemade cart, driven by a youngster about ten. The boy in the picture was David Dains, and this is especially interesting to me since I knew David in later years. He was always interested in animals, and had an assortment of goats, donkeys, ponies, and at one time, a monkey. The cart in the picture is pulled by a billy goat and a Dalmatian dog, "Willie" and "Pepper."

Mr. Dains' sister, who sent me the picture, sent also some information about the team. His biggest problem, she recalls, was finding someone to make a harness. He finally located an old harness marker and persuaded him to make a set of harness for goat and dog for about four dollars.

David's next problem was to get his team to "stand." He had a few runaways before they learned, but from then on, she says, "they were a good team."

The cart looks suspiciously like an old stripped-down dump rake, but may be something that the boy put together from scratch with a pair of old cultivator wheels. At any rate, it looks like a really fun "team."

It hasn't been too many years since some of our kids harnessed our old Irish setter to a sled one winter. They could get up quite a bit of speed, but steering was a little tougher. Mostly they went where Rusty wanted to go, which included over the retaining wall and through the gap in the hedge.

Dogs really are an efficient beast of burden through history. Huskies are still used as sled teams in the frozen north. For that matter, I guess a lot of goats have been used as cart animals, too, though I imagine David Dains' mixed team is a bit unusual.

Mixed teams of various sorts have been used a lot, though. I remember as a boy seeing a lot of farming done with teams consisting of a horse and a mule. This seemed to work fine, but of course isn't as pretty as a nice team of matched Belgians.

The Bible, as part of Mosaic law, warns "Thou shalt not plow with an ox and ass together" (Deuteronomy 22:10). I'm not sure why, although I once wrote an article speculating about it. Anyway, I'm not taking any chances. You won't catch me harnessing any cow and donkey together!

Cattle traditionally make pretty good draft animals, however. The cloven feet of a lot of oxen pulled a lot of covered wagons across the prairie of a century ago. Even into later times, too. I have an old snapshot that my dad took in the 1930's. He was driving in southeast Kansas and saw what was an unusual sight, even for then. The photo plainly shows a team of cattle mowing hay with a sickle bar mower. The really unusual thing is that neither is an ox (a neutered male). The near animal is plainly a milk cow, and the off member of the team is a pretty good-looking Jersey bull!

During the time I spent in the Philippines, I saw a lot of farming done with *carabao*, or water buffalo. Once I even saw a man plowing with his wife and a *carabao* in double harness. Really a mixed team.

That reminds me of an old story about a hillbilly who lost one of his team of mules. He persuaded his wife to fill in. He harnessed the "team" and was just starting to plow when the mule became excited, kicked and plunged, and broke away to run over the hill.

"Catch the mule!" the old lady hollered as she picked herself up. "I'll stand!"

Horsin' Around Again

The Federal Outhouse

One of the zaniest pieces of proposed federal regulation yet came out of the OSHA (Occupational Safety and Health Administration) a couple of years ago. There were provisions to require a handy toilet, with running water for drinking and hand washing, within five minutes' walk of any spot where farm laborers may be employed.

No doubt this legislation was dreamed up by politicians seeking the farm labor vote. It's apparent that the originators never *saw* ranch country, or wheat country. Can you imagine the wide open spaces of the "Lone Prairee" dotted with outhouses (complete with running water, no less)! This will sure be a shock to the cowboy or wheat harvester who hasn't even seen a fence all day.

I can foresee a certain amount of trouble in this. Employers may have to have on application forms questions like "How far can you walk in five minutes?" so they'll know how to space the outhouses. And will employers be subject to prosecution under the equal opportunities act if they refuse to hire a short-legged farmhand because they're afraid he can't make it to the john in five minutes?

What if the facility is located properly for the five minutes' walk of a lanky cowboy. Then ol' Slim quits, and the only available hand is Shorty, who's pretty slow on his feet. What do we do, move the outhouse? Would it be legal to have speed trials prior to employment, similar to those used for typists? A farmhand could carry a card, for instance, certifying his five-minute john-distance as 1.34 miles.

I have a better idea. This will appeal to the politician looking for votes because it should easily attract the votes of the horse industry. Simply this: require employers to supply horses, tethered at intervals throughout the ranch, for the use of interested employees heading for the john. By this means, we could reduce the number of necessary toilets, since a horse could travel much farther in five minutes than a farmhand could walk. By utilizing fast horses, perhaps race-trained animals, the number of biffies could be really reduced, and placed farther apart.

On the other hand, if a farmer wanted to be economical, he could convert to horsepower entirely. The horses used to pull machinery could be the same ones for john duty. One could simply unhitch one of the team, climb aboard, and lope off for the nearest outhouse. (Presumably, all farmhands will be equipped with maps marking locations, anyway.) The plow-horse might be somewhat slower, so johns will have to be spaced closer than in a high-class operation using race-trained thoroughbreds.

Now I'll admit there are a few bugs to be worked out of this scheme yet. First, we'll have to be aware of the risk of losing the toilet manufacturers' votes if we decrease the number required with this horse thing. We'll just have to hope that the votes of the horse breeders' bloc will offset this factor.

Another problem will be, I suppose, that of waste products from the horses themselves. Now I think personally it's no problem, and that a strong case can be made for the ecologic benefits of recyclable organic by-products. In fact, the fertilizer value might easily pay for the cost of the johns.

However, I'm afraid it's not that simple. If you put to work the bureaucratic minds that conceived toilets in the fields (with running water) you have other problems. Sooner or later somebody will object, and a regulation will be proposed to require the horses to wear diapers, or some equally effective measure.

Don't laugh. That has already happened in South Carolina. As Will Rogers said, when the legislature makes a joke, it's a law.

Horsin' Around Again

The Self-Milking Cow

Several people have asked about a foal I wrote about recently. He's doing fine. I think one of the reasons is that his mother, old Raspberry, produces milk like a Holstein cow. Her foals always look good. They're fat and muscular and alert. I don't think there's any substitute for mother's milk to bring a colt along and keep him in top condition. And Raspberry produces plenty of it.

A time or two when we were traveling with Raspberry and her foals, we've had to milk her by hand. This prevented her udder from becoming overfull before we could give the foal a chance to empty it.

Mares' milk is a fine quality product, high in protein and nutrition. Many human babies, in the past, have grown nicely on mares' milk when for some reason or other they couldn't tolerate cows' milk. The horse is a perfect example of efficiency when it comes to converting grass to nutrition for the young.

I don't know why, but this mare and her efficient production started me to thinking about a not so efficient example from my childhood. A neighbor down the road from my uncle's place had two or three milk cows, like most farmers then. One old cow seemed to always have a large, full udder, but he never seemed to get any production out of her. This was his best cow, or should have been, but she never gave nearly as much milk as the others. He finally discovered that she was milking herself. That's not easy for a cow to do, but occasionally does. I read only a couple of years ago about a similar case.

This cow would sort of hump her back, bring front and hind feet as close together as possible, and then raise one hind leg like a dog at a stump. That way she could stretch her head around and manage to get one of her nipples in her mouth.

She apparently accepted the adage that "you never outgrow your need for milk."

Now, while this was sort of entertaining for youngsters to watch, her owner didn't think it was very amusing at all. It was about as funny as the occasional laying hen that learns to break and eat eggs.

Of course, eggs are good nutrition. An egg-eating chicken is usually in good shape, because of all the fine nutrient qualities, the calcium in the shell, and all. It's just that this sort of recycling isn't exactly what the owner has in mind when he buys all that expensive feed.

The same with the self-milking cow. The owner, when he invests in silage, hay, grain, pasture, and supplement, has a right to expect a certain return on his investment. In this case, in milk. My neighbor was getting some milk, of course. Just not what he should. The technique of recycling the product twice lost a great deal in the process. (For some reason this old cow has always reminded me of the federal government.)

The cow stayed fat and happy. Her milk was nutritious and satisfying. But the feed conversion ratio, although nobody was using that expression yet, became pretty unsatisfactory. Eventually the owner realized he couldn't continue to support this situation and remain solvent. The self-milking cow, no matter how good a cow, had to go because he couldn't afford to keep her.

T. Hamilton Bone

When I was in the service during World War II, I took my basic training in one of the last animal units in the U.S. Army. It was a mule artillery unit. More specifically a pack artillery unit. All our guns, ammunition, kitchen gear, and the whole shebang were loaded on pack mules. As my brother says, I served a diamond hitch in the army.

Actually the idea of pack mule artillery was basically a good one. We could take a battery of medium artillery into inaccessible areas where a wheeled vehicle couldn't go. Air power was the nemesis of the mountain pack batteries. You just can't defend a mule train from air attack.

Sundays were usually spent by the mule men at Fort Sill, Oklahoma, in a sort of busman's holiday. We'd ride the mules. There was a big training arena near our barracks. It had a high board fence around it, and was called the "bull pen." It was an ideal place to ride. Bareback of course. We didn't have anything in the way of saddles except the Phillips pack saddle, with various projections for attaching parts of a howitzer.

Now, some might think it's pretty slow stuff to ride a pack mule. Rest assured such is not the case. Some of these old regular army mules were pretty easy-going, but a few really objected to being ridden. On Sunday afternoons we'd have quite a rodeo. One thing that some of the mules loved was jumping. There were odds and ends of equipment still around from when the whole fort was animal-drawn, and we had a few old jumps left. Nobody knew much about formal jumping, but we had a good time, and some of the mules did, too, I think.

I mentioned this a couple of years ago to a friend with a long-time interest in horses and mules, Dick Spencer of *Western Horseman* magazine. Dick told me a mule story that I found a real grabber. He promised to get the details for me and eventually came through.

Hambone was an army mule assigned to Fort Carson, Colorado, in a quartermaster pack unit. He and Trotter, later the West Point mascot, were two of the most famous of army mules, and both served their army duty at Fort Carson. Hambone very early demonstrated his jumping ability, probably in much the same sort of Sunday recreation as our mules at Fort Sill.

The 35th Quartermaster Pack Company was mustered out in 1956, the last animal unit in the army. The mules were sold at auction, and Hambone and Trotter went to J. D. Ackerman of the Pike's Peak or Bust Rodeo. They performed for many years at rodeos, horse shows, and similar functions. Hambone could always be counted on to please a crowd with his jumping exhibitions. Apparently he was all "ham."

In 1970, Ackerman decided to retire the two mules. They were given back to the army. Trotter was sent to West Point as a mascot, and Hambone, now 39 years old, was reassigned to Fort Carson. There he retired in pampered comfort until his death from heart failure in 1971.

But Hambone's most spectacular jumping feat came while he was still on active duty in the army.

One of the biggest events of the year for the horse gentry of the western U.S. is the annual Denver National Western Livestock and Horse Show. There have always been highly competitive jumping classes. One year, about 1950, I believe, the soldiers at Fort Carson got to thinking what a joke it would be to enter old Hambone in the show. One thing led to another, and by means of various skulduggery, they managed to enter the old pack mule, already nearly twenty years old, in the jumping contest. He appeared on the program as T. Hamilton Bone, from Fort Carson.

The old white mule ran the course perfectly, completing without a fault, and the army explained that it had all been a joke.

Funny, though. Some of the owners of the high-priced jumpers didn't think it was funny at all.

Nature's Fertilizer

We've just come through a pretty tough winter. About the worst in the memory of man, in fact. One consolation, although a pretty thin one, is that most places in the country had it even worse than we did. At least we don't have to live in California. My suspicions that they have the country's worst weather were recently confirmed. A CBS news item showed a sign being changed. The old sign was taken down, "Drought Relief Station" and replaced with one that said "Flood Relief Station." Same office and personnel. They just change the sign to conform to their current emergency. It made me glad once again to live in the Kansas Flint Hills.

Still, I don't remember in my lifetime any winter when we had continuous snow cover for so long. About every time it looked like the weather would open up and we'd get a little springtime, it seemed that it would be back-ordered once more.

Not that snow isn't beneficial. Any wheat farmer or rancher with extensive pastures will understand that. In the places where the deepest drifts stood in the winter, the wheat or grass will be the tallest and most lush and green. I think it took a lot of years to understand why. It couldn't be the moisture involved. That's soon dissipated. Somebody finally figured out that it's nitrogen. We can apply nitrogen chemically to our fields, but nature does it with snow. And if this is any real help, we ought to really have great wheat and grass this year. As an added bonus, the fall growth of native grass was the best in many years. That standing hay will have caught and held a lot of snow to provide nutrition for the coming season.

All of which reminds me of a story I heard recently. One of the local service station operators is a farm boy by background. At the height of the snow season, he had piles of snow out on his drive six or eight feet high. It was a difficult thing to even keep the drive clear enough for cars to get to the gas pumps. This even without all the demand for help with chains, antifreeze, dead batteries, and so on. He was about to think there may have been better lines of work to have entered.

Into the midst of all this there drove a customer one morning who was a sort of Jesus-freak of the pro-ecology, back-to-nature persuasion. Our friend the service man was complaining bitterly about all the snow. He was reprimanded by his customer. You shouldn't feel that way, he was told. Don't you know the snow is one of God's blessings? Our friend said nothing. Having a captive audience, the nature boy warmed to his subject.

Snow, he explained, falling from the sky, gathers unto itself nitrogen. It falls softly on the earth, replenishing the soil, rejuvenating all living things. Thus, when spring comes, all plants can awake with renewed vigor, with nutrients available for the year's growth.

"So, you see," he summed up, "the snow really is God's fertilizer!"

Our half-frozen service man looked from his ice-covered pumps to the mountains of snow on his station drives.

"Well," he said slowly, "so is chicken manure. But I just don't want it all over me!"

The Cribber

We recently kept our 18-month-old grandson for the weekend while his parents were out of town. Our old baby crib was getting a little decrepit after a series of occupants, so we borrowed a newer model.

I was pleased to see that it was equipped with a plastic guard rail all around the top edge to prevent chewing. Nathan has chawed his own crib pretty dramatically, and I'd have hated to return this borrowed bed with fresh tooth marks.

It's interesting that some youngsters chew the rail of their crib more than others. I suppose it's because of the variation in the way their front teeth come in. There's no definite order about it, but usually there are two up and two down, which gives a bite like a rodent for awhile. Thus a lot of cribs look like a beaver has been after them. Some families even highly prize a piece of furniture with the tooth marks of one of the kids, now grown, departed, rich, and famous.

While I was pondering all this and thinking that chewing the crib is a pretty universal thing among youngsters, another thought suddenly struck me. Some horses do the same thing. They'll chew, and even destroy, fence boards, stall dividers, feed boxes, and anything made of wood. And a horse that does this sort of chewing is called, of all things, a "cribber." Well, get right down to thinking about it, it's pretty obvious where that name comes from.

Why does a cribber crib? I've heard a lot of explanations that ranged from problems with the teeth to vitamin deficiencies. My own personal feeling is that it's usually boredom. A horse in a stall or small pen with nothing to do will start to chew just from lack of anything better. I've seen some pretty good horsemen hang a plastic milk jug on a string from the rafters in the barn, just for a horse to play with. He'd sort of bump it around with his nose, and it seemed to help keep him from chewing. Painting the wood with creosote helps, too.

But occasionally there's a horse that just seems to have a pathologic urge to bite into wood. Other words besides cribber are "stump-sucker" and "wind-sucker" for these animals. I've heard them called other things, too, by their owners. They will bite so hard into a two-by-six board that they break teeth and bloody their gums. The "wind-sucker" nomenclature comes from the fact that some of these horses will noisily inhale while they're biting down.

About the only cure for this severe a case seems to be a strap around the neck. Most generally a belt about two inches wide is buckled pretty snugly around the throat just behind the jawbones. For reasons I don't pretend to understand, this prevents the cribbing.

A few years ago we were traveling in another part of the country and stopped to see an acquaintance who was campaigning a well-known stallion. We'd seen this horse in the ring a good many times, but never in an informal setting. We pulled into the yard, and our friend waved to us from the barn so we walked on down there. A horse "spoke" from the stall just inside, and I just naturally looked around the corner. There stood the famous stallion with a leather belt around his throatlatch. He was a cribber! I never mentioned it, and neither did our friend.

Gatherin' Sunbeams

Aesop's Horse

I'm a pipe smoker. My wife says I'm actually a match smoker, because I get distracted, my pipe goes out, and I use up a whole batch of matches before I discover that the tobacco is all burned up anyway. I think what she likes best about all this is the glorious way a pipe smells when I'm trying to relight the tar and ashes in the bottom.

Anyway, I asked her to bring some matches next time she went to the store. There are a lot of really attractive match folders on the market any more, and the box she brought was labeled "Parables." It was a collection of little truisms such as we grew up with, like "A rolling stone gathers no moss", "A fool and his money are soon parted", and "A stitch in time saves nine." (I never did understand that last one, and it's not even a good rhyme.) And, of course, the old one about looking a gift horse in the mouth.

These homey little sayings were a part of education a generation ago. They taught morals and ethics, and were quoted endlessly and worked into samplers until kids were sick of them. My own grandmother never seemed to encounter a situation that did not call for a quotation. A little bragging about a good report card brought forth "Pride goeth before a fall." My sister got: "Whistling girls and crowing hens
    Always come to some bad ends."
It was okay. She couldn't whistle much, anyhow.

Recalling, though, how important this sort of thing was in a youngster's education, I thought of a book I was given as a child, *Aesop's Fables*. This was much the same principle. These animal stories, each with a moral, actually date from several hundred years before Christ. Aesop was a slave, but his wit and wisdom still can make us chuckle and realize that nothing ever changes much. Some of the morals have become part of our culture. Everyone knows what is meant by "sour grapes" and what constitutes a "dog-in-the-manger" attitude. Aesop may have had a profound effect on Western civilization.

Of course, many of his fables deal with horses and donkeys.

175

Horsin' Around Again

I was glancing over some of the old stories and spotted a couple of significance.

A Horse had the plain all to himself, but his domain was encroached upon by a Stag. He asked Man for help against the intruder. Man agreed, and suggested that he ride upon the Horse, guiding by a bit in the Horse's mouth. The Stag was vanquished by this scheme, but ever since, the Horse has been slave to Man.

Or another: On a cold night, an Ox, a Horse, and a Dog asked shelter. Man took them in, cared for, and fed them. To repay Man, they divided the term of his life between them, each endowing one portion of it with his own qualities.

Ever since, Man has, in his youth, been like the Horse: strong willed, obstinate, and impetuous. In middle years he is like the Ox: plodding, hardworking, striving to produce. In old age, he is like the Dog: snappish, irritable, distrustful of strangers, and hard to please.

Apparently Aesop never had a very nice dog. Or a very good horse, either, I guess.

The Tractor Speaks

I was talking with a couple of other horsemen recently about the conversion from horsepower to tractor power back in the 1930's. We each had our own memories of that era and were sort of swapping stories.

I mentioned that I had once heard a group of farmers arguing the relative merits of horses vs. tractors. One became quite irate. There was just no way, he insisted, that a man could farm without at least one team of "work horses." Where, he demanded of the others, would you get your fertilizer? He then stalked off, satisfied that he had put the others in their place with the final argument.

Actually, we hear increasingly about farms here and there that are operated partially or entirely with horses. I really think it's on the increase. Some of the pulling-horse people use their teams for some of their farming to keep the animals in shape. A lot of them, though, use horses for field work because they like it. The living response of a heavy draft team is far more of a thrill to drive than the mechanical reaction of a noisy tractor.

And a team can help you, too. My dad used to tell about going to help out his father-in-law, who was ill. The corn needed cultivating, and my dad, who was pretty much an amateur, was having a bit of trouble. He was fighting the team constantly, and tearing up about as much corn as he cultivated. Especially was this true on the turns at the end of the field. Finally, in desperation, he sort of let the old mares have their heads.

Much to his surprise, they settled down to work calmly and steadily. They weren't spoiling any more corn, and took the turns at the end cleanly and efficiently. By the time my grandfather was back on his feet, the farm was running pretty well again. It must be frustrating to a good team to have to break in a new driver.

One thing that's pretty universally true is that horsemen talk to a team that they're driving. Some sing or just carry on a rambling conversation. The horses seem to appreciate it. Well, sometimes you have to cuss 'em a little, too.

Then there are some horses that initiate the conversation. We have one mare who does this. In the sixteen years or so that we've had her, I've never stepped into her range of sight that she didn't raise her head and "speak" to me. A couple of her daughters have this same characteristic. It's sort of flattering, I guess.

If we speak to her, this mare answers, too. It's a comfortable feeling to have a horse nicker softly from a dark barn on a chilly night when you step inside. I can't recall that I ever had a tractor do that. They just stand there cold and smelly and greasy and unattractive.

I made that sort of a statement to the horsemen I was talking to, and one of them chuckled. He well remembered the first tractor his dad bought, he said. As a teenager, he was thrilled to be driving the brand new machine. Obviously it was much superior to the outmoded horses they'd been driving. He could hardly wait to get to the field to try it out.

The tractor worked well. He didn't have to fight the team. The pull across the cornfield was smooth and effortless and he knew that this was really going to make his life easy. In fact, he felt so good that as he approached the end of the rows, he was relaxed and singing to the tractor, as he always did to the team.

There was one difference, however. The tractor didn't seem to notice when it was time to turn around. It kept on straight ahead. In fact, although he was pulling back hard on the steering wheel and hollering "whoa" at the top of his lungs, the tractor was still going straight ahead when it went through the fence.

How They Get the Milk Out

A number of years ago, before the Appaloosa was a well-known breed, we had some friends who were raising and showing them extensively. Some of the questions they got were amazing. People would come by the stall or grooming area and ask such things as "what kind of paint do you use to put the spots on?"

I guess asking questions is the way to learn, but golly, sometimes it looks like a hopeless goal. When somebody oriented in one field or one socioeconomic group comes in contact with another, they may not even speak the same language. Somebody at a horse show once asked us how we take the horse's shoes off at night.

We recently had a letter from our daughter April on the ranch in Colorado. She was telling about a recent evening where three ranch couples were together. They were recalling some of the odd remarks, questions, and so on that they had heard from non-country people. I would have loved to have been there, but even secondhand, some of these were choice.

One of the girls told about a city-raised friend who was buying a half of beef to put in the freezer. With delight, the purchaser was talking of all the delicious steaks, roasts, and hamburger that would fill their freezer with provisions enough for the whole year. She was doing fine until she expressed a hope that there would be plenty of bacon among the various cuts.

Well, the first storyteller never has a chance of course. Another couple told about some visitors one summer who were impressed by all the windmills in the area. In nearly every pasture was a place where the cattle liked to stand, around the water tank, while the windmill busily whirled overhead. Come to find out, after much comment, that the visitors had a sort of distorted idea of the whole thing. It seems they didn't exactly understand the principle of using wind energy to pump water for the stock. (I don't know where they thought the water came from.)

Apparently they had the idea that the windmill was put there because that's where the cows gathered, around the tank. The purpose of the windmill they perceived as a humanitarian thing. These folks actually thought the busily turning mills were fans to cool the cows on a hot afternoon.

Well, if the first storyteller hasn't a chance, the second isn't much better off. The next story is bound to top even that. The third couple shook out their loop and began.

Visitors had been at a ranch where they were preparing to work some cattle. The city folks were anxious to watch firsthand the work of real cowboys. Consequently, they were escorted to the working corral where the cattle were being brought in.

I'm not sure what sort of operation was in progress, but it involved moving a number of animals through the corral for branding or dehorning or such. It was a well-equipped corral, with a working chute and a squeeze at the end.

The first animal came through, down the alleyway, and into the chute. The headgate locked around the neck, and somebody threw the lever. The sides of the chute closed around the cow, squeezing it firmly.

"Oh," exclaimed the city girl, "so that's how you get the milk out!"

The Thirsty Phantom

I have a friend who is a professional man with a lifelong interest in ranching. He has a small cattle operation, which he uses as a sort of escape from the pressures of dealing with people. On his day off, he can be found working calves or fixing fence or doing the other hundred chores involved in a farm or ranch. But he's outdoors, and he's happy at this second job. It doesn't pay very well, but it's definitely not a tax write-off for him. (Incidentally, I've always felt that you can tell a guy using a ranch for a tax shelter by one simple test: does he shovel his own manure?)

My friend had a couple of young heifers in a small pasture, and, like a lot of the rest of us this year, was short of water. He moved a galvanized stock tank into the pasture, and by stringing out enough garden hose, was able to fill the tank through the fence.

Next morning when he went out to check the heifers, the tank was empty. Must have a leak, he thought, but the ground wasn't muddy. Puzzled, he refilled the tank. For a day or two, no problems. The water level remained nearly full, just the amount missing that you'd expect a couple of animals to drink.

But then a few days later came another morning with the tank bone dry. He moved the empty tank and looked for rat holes in the ground where water could be lost, assuming there was a leak in the tank. He turned the tank over, inspected the bottom, then got under it to look for pinhole leaks against the sunlight. Nothing. He replaced the tank and refilled it. Next morning it was empty again.

Now he became a bit concerned. Could some other livestock

be crawling through the fence and out again? He checked and tightened the entire pasture fence, although he felt a little foolish about it. It was obvious that it would take a whole herd of steers to drink the 150 gallons or so of water overnight. He even thought of other animals that could account for the missing water. An elephant, perhaps, reaching across the fence in the night? He went so far as to look for tracks, but was still a bit too embarrassed to actually inquire if anyone was missing an elephant.

The whole thing was getting a little spooky. Some mornings the water level seemed untouched, but on others, at completely random intervals, the tank would be dry.

The mystery was really beginning to bother him. He checked the tank again for leaks. None. The possibility of one of the calves climbing into the tank and overflowing it was rejected. There had not been, at any time, any evidence of wetness around or under the tank. I'm sure that the thought must have crossed his mind that he was hallucinating, or about to have a mental break of some sort. Had he *really* filled it last night? Or did he just intend to? No, that couldn't be it. It had happened too many times.

He seriously considered spending the night at the tank just to see what was happening. Anything to set the mystery at rest. He told me later that while he has never really believed in ghosts, he was ready to consider the supernatural. Maybe the poltergeist phenomenon, where inanimate objects are moved mysteriously.

Then one evening as he walked over to connect the hose, he noticed there was mud under his feet. Not at the tank, but near the frostproof faucet where the hose attached. He did a little experimenting and in a matter of minutes the mystery was solved. When he left the hose connected, the tank remained full. If he disconnected at the faucet and dropped the hose on the ground, the tank and hose created a siphon. The water ran backwards, out of the tank and onto the ground near the faucet. This would take only a few minutes, and would be pretty well dissipated by the time he'd come around next morning.

Well, he felt better about it, but I sort of thought it was more fun when it was a mystery.

The Grass is Greener

Horsin' Around Again

A few years ago one of the horse magazines had an outstanding cover painting. It was an informal pasture setting, with a barbwire fence running through the center of the scene. There were a couple of horses on each side of the fence. Horses will congregate this way in adjacent pastures. I suppose, being herd animals by nature, they just naturally seek others of their own kind. They will hang around for hours, apparently just visiting or enjoying each others' company.

The thing about this picture, however, was that two of the horses were grazing next to the fence. Each animal had his head between the strands of wire, neck stretched to the fullest, cropping grass on the other side of the fence. But these horses were in different pastures, and each was eating on the opposite side, in the other's grass. A perfect illustration of the old adage about the grass is always greener there.

This picture struck me especially because I've seen our own horses do this. We have a wire fence that divides the pasture behind the house, and more than once I've chuckled to see them stretching and straining to reach a few blades of grass on the other side. They might have even better graze on their own side but it isn't the same.

Even in a pasture with plenty of grass, most horses will eat, first and by preference, grass along, under, and across the fence.

Actually, I guess people are pretty much the same way. There's a great tendency to think the other guy has a better thing going than we do. We figure we'd really be fixed up fine if we had what *he* does. When I was a little kid we'd watch one of the local high-rollers drive past in his big black Packard, and some kid would say,

"Boy, I wish I had that car and he was settin' on a feather! Then we'd both be tickled!"

We have such a tendency to envy the other guy's possession of his house, car, job, status, and all the rest, that there are very early Biblical injunctions against this sort of feeling. "Thou shalt not covet." Of course, there's nothing wrong with wanting something *like* his. We're just not supposed to want *his*.

There are very practical reasons for *not* wanting what the other guy has. Another old saying goes something like this:

"Choose with care what you passionately desire. You might get it."

In other words, maybe the guy with the big car, house, and all, isn't really so much better off than the rest of us. We don't know whether he has problems with a leaky roof, or high fuel bills for that poorly insulated monster. His big car may be a real lemon, and is at least probably a gas guzzler. His soft, high-paying job may have so many problems that he's developing ulcers. Even his expensive-looking wife may actually be a real shrew to live with.

We don't really know all the other guy's problems. He works hard at concealing them, just as we all work hard at concealing ours. I think sometimes we're all engaged in a colossal game of trying to conceal all our problems from the rest of the world.

There's an American Indian saying, "Never judge a man until you have walked a month in his moccasins," which is a perceptive way of saying the same thing.

So, the grass is always greener on the other side of the fence. In my case, it is always greener (and grows faster, too) on the lawn side, where I have to mow it, than on the pasture side, where I need it for the horses.

And why does a horse with perfectly good graze on his side of the fence want to reach through for grass on the other side? Just human nature, I guess.

See you down the road.

DON COLDSMITH is a physician in family practice at Emporia, Kansas. He is also a breeder of registered Appaloosa horses, a newspaper columnist, and published novelist. He is a contributing editor of *Horse Of Course!*, the world's second largest horse publication, where most of the articles in this book were first printed. His weekly newspaper column "Horsin' Around" is published regularly in four states.

Having always had an interest in horses, Don is active in 4H work and in various saddle club activities. He has been a breed inspector for the national Appaloosa Horse Club and a judge in the horsemanship phase of the Miss Rodeo Kansas contest. Don and Edna Coldsmith raise Appaloosa horses but "like all kinds." They have also raised five daughters — all horsewomen.

During World War II, Don was in one of the last U.S. Army artillery units to be transported by mules. He saw action in the Philippines as a combat medic, and assisted in the medical care of such notable war prisoners as Japanese Premier Tojo and General Homma.

This book was designed by Paul Hudgins,
set in 11 point Plantin by Smith & Pettit, Inc.
of San Antonio and printed on Warren's Olde Style Uncoated Book
by Best Printing Co. of Austin.

Property of
Stewartville High School